Blue Marlin

Blue Marlin

LEE SMITH

BLAIR

Printed in the United States of America
Cover design by Hannah Lee
Interior design by April Leidig

Blair is an imprint of Carolina Wren Press.

*The mission of Blair / Carolina Wren Press is to seek out, nurture,
and promote literary work by new and underrepresented writers.*

We gratefully acknowledge the ongoing support of general operations
by the Durham Arts Council's United Arts Fund.

Library of Congress Control Number: 2020930238
ISBN: 978-1-949467-31-4

*For movie lovers
and romantics everywhere—
especially Hal,
my leading man*

Blue Marlin

I N 1958, WHEN my father had his famous affair with Carroll Byrd, I knew it before anybody. I don't know how long he'd been having the affair before I found out about it—or, to be exact, before I realized it. Before it came over me. One day I was riding my bike all over town the way I always did, and the next day I was riding my bike all over town *knowing it*, and this knowledge gave an extra depth, a heightened dimension and color, to everything. Before, I'd been just any old thirteen-year-old girl on a bike. Now I was a *girl whose father was having an affair*—a tragic girl, a dramatic girl. A girl with a burning secret. Everything was different.

All my conversations, especially my conversations with my mother, became almost electrical, charged with hidden import: "pregnant with meaning," in the lingo of the love magazines and movie magazines she was constantly reading. Well, okay, *we* were constantly reading. For my mother loved the lives of the stars above all else. She hated regular newspapers. She hated facts. She also hated club meetings, housework, politics, business, and her mother-in-law. She was not civic. She adored shopping, friends, cooking, gardening, dancing, children and babies and kittens (all little helpless things, actually), and my father. Especially she adored my father. Mama's favorite word was "sweet." She'd cry at the drop of a hat, and kept a clump of pink Kleenex tucked into her bosom at all times, just in case. She called people "poor souls."

That spring, Elizabeth Taylor was the poorest soul around, when Mike Todd was killed in a plane crash one week before the Academy Awards. Elizabeth, clutching their tiny baby, Liza, was in shock as her Hollywood and New York friends rallied to her side. The industry had never seen such a dynamo as Todd, whose electric energy sparked everyone. Just a few weeks before Todd's death, he had celebrated Elizabeth's twenty-sixth birthday by giving her a dazzling diamond necklace at the Golden Globe Awards dinner.

Not a "poor soul" was Ava Gardner, who had divorced Frank Sinatra for the Italian actor Walter Chiari and now was trying to steal Shelley Winters's husband, Anthony Franciosa, playing opposite her in *The Naked Maja*, currently being filmed in Rome.

"Can you *imagine*?" My mother, clutching *Photoplay*, was outraged. "Isn't Ava ever satisfied? Just think how Shelley Winters must feel!"

"It's terrible," I agreed. *If you only knew*, I thought. I sat down on the edge of the chaise lounge to peer at the pictures of Ava and Shelley and Tony in a Roman nightclub.

"Look at that *dress*." Mama pointed to Ava.

"What a bitch," I said loyally. *If you only knew*, I thought.

"Honestly, Jenny, such language!" But Mama was giggling. "I don't know what I'm going to do with you."

Nothing, was the answer to that, already clear to both of us. The fact is, I was just too much for Mama, coming along to them so late in life (a "surprise"), after my two older sisters had already "sapped her strength" and "lowered her resistance," as she said, to all kinds of things, including migraine headaches, asthma, and a heart murmur. These ailments required her to lie down a lot but did not prevent her from being perfectly beautiful, as always.

My mother was widely known as one of the most beautiful women in Virginia, everybody said so. Previously she had been the most beautiful girl in Charleston, South Carolina, where she had grown up as Billie Rutledge and lived until she married my father, John Fitzhugh Dale, Jr., a naval officer stationed there briefly during the war. "Just long enough to sweep me off my feet," as she put it. He was a divine dancer, and my most cherished image of my parents involved them waltzing grandly around a ballroom floor, she in a long white gown, he in a snappy uniform, her hair and the buttons on the uniform gleaming golden in the light from the sparkling chandeliers.

Thus she became Billie Rutledge Dale, in a ceremony I loved to imagine. It was a wedding of superlatives: the handsomest couple in the world, a wedding cake six feet high, a gown with a train fifteen feet long, ten bridesmaids, a horse and buggy—not to mention a former suitor's suicide attempt the night before, while everybody else was dancing the night away at the rehearsal dinner. I was especially fascinated by this unsuccessful project, which had involved the young man's trying to hang himself from a coat rack in a downtown men's club, after which he was forever referred to as Bobby "Too Tall" Burkes.

Some people said Mama looked like Marilyn Monroe, but I didn't think so; Mama was bigger, blonder, paler, softer, with a sort of inflatable celluloid prettiness. She looked like a great big baby doll. People also said I took after Mama, but this wasn't true, either, at least not yet, and I didn't want it to become true, at least not entirely, as I feared that taking after her too much might eventually damn me into lying down a lot of the time, which looked pretty boring.

On the other hand, I was simply dying to get my period, grow breasts, turn into a sexpot, and do as much damage as Mama, who had broken every heart in Charleston and had a charm bracelet made out of fraternity pins to prove it. She used to tick them off for me one by one. "Now that was Smedes Black, a Phi Delt from UVA, such a darling boy, and this one was Parker Winthrop, a Sigma Chi at W and L, he used to play the ukulele . . ." I was drunk on the sound of so many alphabetical syllables. My mother had "come out" in Charleston; my sisters had attended St. Catherine's School and then "come out" in Richmond, since nobody did such a thing in Lewisville, outside Lynchburg, where we lived. I was expected to follow in my sisters' footsteps.

But then our paths would diverge, as I secretly planned to go up north to college before becoming (to everyone's total astonishment) a *writer*. First I would write steamy novels about my own hot love life, eventually getting world-famous like Grace Metalious. I would make millions of dollars and give it all away to starving children in foreign lands. I would win the Nobel Prize. Then I would become a vegetarian poet in Greenwich Village. I would live for Art.

I had a big future ahead of me. But so far, nothing doing. No breasts, no period, no sex, no art. Though very blonde, I was just any skinny, pale, wispy-haired kid on a bike, quick as a rabbit, fast as a bird, riding invisible all over town, bearing my awful secret.

I KNEW WHO SHE was, of course. Everyone knew. Her father, Old Man Byrd, had been the county judge for forty years. After retirement, he became a hermit—or as close to a hermit as it was possible to be in Lewisville, which was chock-full of neighborly curious people naturally bound and determined to look after one another all the time. ("I swear to God," my father remarked once in exasperation, "if the devil himself moved into this town, I guess you'd take *him* a casserole, too!") Judge Byrd was a wild-looking, white-haired, ugly old man whose eyebrows grew all the way across his face in the most alarming fashion; he walked bent over, leaning on a walking stick topped by a carved ivory skull, yelling at children. He smelled bad. He did not socialize. He did not go to church, and was rumored to be an atheist. When he died, everyone was shocked to learn that there would be *no funeral*, unheard of in our town. Furthermore, he was to be *cremated*.

I remember the conversation Mama and Daddy had about it at the time.

"Cremated . . ." Mama mused. "Isn't that sort of . . . communist? Don't they do it in Russia and places like that?"

"Lord, no, honey." Daddy was laughing. "It's perfectly common, in this country as well as abroad. For one thing, it's a lot more economical."

"Well, it certainly isn't *southern*," Mama sniffed. "And I certainly don't intend to have it done to *me*. Are you listening, John? I want my body to remain as intact as possible, and I want to be buried with all my rings on. And a nice suit, or maybe a dress with a little matching jacket. And I want lots of yellow roses, as in life."

"Yes, Billie." Daddy hid a smile as he went out the door. He was Old Man Byrd's lawyer, and so was in charge of the arrangements. I couldn't believe my own daddy was actually getting to go inside Old Man Byrd's house, a vine-covered mansion outside town, which everyone called "The Ivy House." But of course my father *was* the best lawyer in town, so it followed that he'd be the judge's lawyer, too. And since he was the soul of discretion, it also followed that he'd never mentioned this to us, not even when my cousin Jinx and I got caught trying to peep in Old Man Byrd's windows on a dare. I still remember what we saw: a gloomy sitting room full of dark, crouching furniture; a fat white cat on a chair; the housekeeper's sudden furious face.

Jinx and I were grounded from our bikes for a whole week, during which I completed a paint-by-numbers version of Leonardo da Vinci's *Last Supper*, done mostly in shades of orange and gold, and presented it to my daddy, who seemed surprised.

"I'm sorry for trespassing," I said. "I'll never do it again."

But I wasn't sorry, not in the least. The incident marked the beginning of my secret career.

I lived to spy, and this was mainly what I did on my bike trips around town. I'd seen some really neat stuff, too. For instance, I had seen Roger Ainsley, the coolest guy in our school, squeezing pimples in his bathroom mirror. I'd seen Mr. Bondurant whip his big son Earl with a belt a lot harder than anybody ever ought to, and later, when Earl dropped out of school and enlisted in the Army, I alone knew why. I had seen my fourth-grade teacher, prissy Miss Emily Horn, necking on the couch with her boyfriend and smoking cigarettes. Best of all, I had seen Mrs. Cecil Hertz come running past a picture window wearing nothing but an apron, followed shortly by Mr. Cecil Hertz himself, wearing nothing at all and carrying a spatula.

It was amazing how careless people were about drawing their drapes and pulling their shades down. It was amazing what you could see, especially if you were an athletic and enterprising girl such as myself. I wrote my observations down in a Davy Crockett spiral notebook I'd bought for this purpose. I wrote down everything: date, time, weather, physical descriptions, my reaction. I would use this stuff later, in my novels.

I saw Carroll Byrd the very first time I rode out there to spy on her, after the old man's death. It was a cold gray day in January, and she was burning trash. The sky was so dark that I didn't notice the smoke at first, not until I was halfway down the long lane that went from the road to the house—her house, now. In spite of the cold, she had opened the windows, flung the shutters outward, and left the front door wide open, too. Airing everything out, I guessed. The whole house wore a rattled, astonished expression. She had a regular bonfire going on the patio in the side yard—cardboard boxes, newspapers, old magazines. She emerged from the house with armful after armful of old papers to feed the yellow flames.

I had ditched my bike earlier, up the lane; now I dodged behind giant boxwoods, getting closer and closer. This was interesting. Neither my mother nor any of her friends would *ever* have acted like Carroll Byrd. In the first place, they all had constant help and never lifted a finger carrying any-thing. In the second place, Mama "would not be found dead" dressed the way Carroll Byrd was dressed that day: she wore work boots, just like a field hand; men's pants belted at the waist; and a tight, long-sleeved black sweater (*leotard* was a word I would not learn until college). Her dark hair, longer than any woman's in town, was pulled back severely from her high forehead and tied with a string, and fell straight down her back. Indian hair, streaked with gray. I knew instinctively that she didn't care about the gray, that she would never color it. Nor would she ever wear makeup. Her face was lean and hard, her cheekbones chiseled. She had inherited her father's heavy brows, like dark wings about the deep-set black eyes.

While I watched, she paused in the middle of one of her

trips to the house, and my heart leaped up to my throat as I thought that I had been discovered. But no. Carroll Byrd had stopped to eye an ornate white trellis, nonfunctional but pretty, which arched over the path between the house and the patio. Hand on hip, she considered it. She walked around it. Then, before I could believe what she was doing, she ripped it out of the ground and was breaking it up like so many matchsticks, throwing the pieces into the fire. Red flames shot toward the lowering sky. She laughed out loud. I noted her generous mouth, the flash of white teeth.

Then Carroll Byrd sat down on an iron bench to watch her fire burn for a while. She lit a cigarette, striking the match on her boot. Now I noticed that she wasn't wearing a brassiere, something I had read about but never seen done among "nice" women. When she leaned over to stub out her cigarette on the patio tiles, I saw her breasts shift beneath the black sweater. Immediately I thought of "Selena's brown nipples" on page 72 in Jinx's and my dog-eared, hidden copy of *Peyton Place*. I was both disgusted and thrilled.

There in the cramped and pungent safety of the giant boxwood bush, I fell in love. We watched her fire, the two of us from our different vantage points, until it burned itself out. She ran a hose on the ashes before she went inside her father's house and shut the door.

I sneaked back to my bike and rode down the long lane and then home, pedaling as fast as I could, freezing to death. But my own house seemed too warm, too bright, too soft—now I hated the baby-blue shag rug in my room, hated all my stuffed animals. I wanted fire and bare trees and cold gray sky. I went straight to bed and wouldn't get up for dinner. After a while, Mama came in and took my temperature (normal) and brought me a bowl of milk toast on a tray. This was what you got in our house when you were sick, and it was delicious.

MAMA WAS A great cook. She also loved to talk on the phone, and during the next weeks, I strained to overhear any mention of Carroll Byrd. I got plenty of material. But since Mama generally stayed home and was the recipient rather than the purveyor of news, it was sometimes hard for me to figure out what had actually happened.

"She *what*?"

"You're kidding! Why, those rugs are worth a fortune! That furniture came from England!"

"Oh, he did *not*!"

"Well, that is the strangest thing I have ever heard in my whole life. The strangest!"

"You're kidding!"

Et cetera.

I had to decipher the news: Carroll Byrd had given away the downstairs furnishings and the Oriental rugs to several distant relations, who showed up in U-Hauls to claim them and cart them away. Then she fired the housekeeper. She hired Norman Estep, a local ne'er-do-well and jack-of-all-trades, to knock down the walls between the kitchen and the dining room and the parlor, and paint everything white, including "that beautiful paneling." ("Have you *ever*?") Next, several huge wooden crates arrived for Carroll Byrd from Maine, and Norman went to the train station and picked them up in his truck and took them to her house.

For Carroll Byrd was a painter, it developed. Not a house-painter, of course, but the other kind—an *artist*. The minute I heard this, a long shudder ran from the top of my head to my feet. An *artist*. Of course! She had decided to stay on in her father's house because she loved the light down here as spring came on.

"The what?' Mama asked, puckering up her mouth as she talked on the phone to Jinx's mother. "I mean, it's light up in Maine, too, isn't it?"

Well, yes, but Carrol Byrd feels that there is a *special quality* to the light here in Virginia that she just has to capture on canvas. So now Norman Estep is building frames, huge frames, for her canvases. And now he's going all around to junk yards for pieces of iron, and now he's buying welding tools at Southern States Supply. For her *sculptures*—turns out she's a sculptor, too. Newly elevated to a position of importance by his privileged relationship with Carroll Byrd, Norman Estep is grilled mercilessly by all the women in town, and clams up. Now he won't tell anybody anything. Neither what she's painting, nor what she wears, nor what in the world she does out there all day long by herself. Norman Estep buys groceries for her in the Piggly Wiggly, consulting a list penned in a stark angular hand. He won't even tell anybody what she eats! He is completely loyal to Carroll Byrd.

But the women turn against her. They drive out there to welcome her, two by two, carrying cakes or pies or casseroles or congealed salad, to be met cordially at the door by the artist herself, who does not ask them in. She responds politely to their questions but does not initiate any topics herself. Finally, in some consternation, the women turn on their heels and lurch off down the long walk, but not before noticing that she's made a huge mess of the patio—why, it's got an old iron gate and pieces of junk from the junkyard piled right in the middle of it, some of them welded together into this awful-looking construction that Mama swears is a human figure but Jinx's mama says is no such thing—and not before seeing that Carroll Byrd's gotten Norman Estep to plow up all that pretty grass in front of the house for a big vegetable garden, of all things! No lady has a vegetable garden, and no person in their right mind would put such a garden *in front* of a nice house, anyway. ("Lovely home," Mama always says.)

Several weeks after accepting the food, Carroll Byrd sends Norman around to deliver the plates and containers back to their original owners, each with its terse little thank-you note attached, written on fine creamy paper with raised initials.

This paper seems to make Mama madder than anything yet. ("I'll swear! It's certainly not like she *doesn't know any better*.") By then it is clear to all that Carroll Byrd is determined to be as much of a hermit as her father was, even more of one, and in the way of small towns, everybody stops badgering her and even begins to take a perverse pride in her eccentricity. "See that long driveway goes right up that way?" a visitor might be told. "There's a world-famous woman artist lives up there all by herself. Never goes past the gate."

BUT MOST PEOPLE, including Mama, forgot about Carroll Byrd as spring turned into summer and more recent events claimed everyone's attention. Susan Blackwelder had a miscarriage, then fell into a depression; old Mr. Bishop retired and then sold his downtown Commercial Hotel to two young men from Washington who were reputed to be "homos," which interested me, naturally, and led to some fascinating observations. Best of all, Miss Lavinia Doolittle knelt *but never ros*e from taking Communion at the altar in the Episcopal church on Palm Sunday. She *died* with her wafer in her mouth. I loved this, and was furious that we had missed it by attending the eleven-o'clock service rather than the nine-o'clock, just because Mama always said nine o'clock was "too early for God or anybody."

Still, *I* didn't forget about Carroll Byrd. I rode my bike about once a week all summer long, with time off for camp and Bible school and the beach. I'd usually find her outside, wearing a halter and cutoff jeans, working in the garden with her braided hair wound on top of her head. She was brown as a berry, strong as a man. The garden thrived, with shiny red tomatoes and big-leafed tropical-looking squash plants and enormous sunflowers that nodded on their stalks like happy idiots. I could have stepped right up and spoken to her, and often I thought I *would*, but somehow I never did. One time she put a plateful of fresh vegetables from the garden on a table outdoors and set up an easel to paint them. I couldn't see the painting, but I could see her face: dire, ruthless, beautiful.

It stayed with me all summer while I went off to 4-H camp and then Camp Nantahala and then to Virginia Beach with my mother and Jinx and Jinx's mother. Virginia Beach was loud and bright and fun, though Jinx and I were dismayed to find that a boy from our very own class back in Lewisville, Buddy Womble, was staying down the beach, and would not let us alone. He liked to sneak up on us while we were lying out in the sun with little wet pads of cotton over our eyes, as suggested by *Teen* magazine. "Gotcha!" Buddy Womble would holler, kicking sand, which stuck to our baby-oiled arms and legs and made us look like sandpaper girls. Then he'd run off down the beach laughing his big fake laugh, "Har-dee-har-har," at the top of his lungs. Jinx and I hated him. We went spying on his cottage one night and were appalled to witness Buddy's fat father, sitting alone on the porch, bury his face in his hands and sob as if his heart would break. This violated every known rule of conduct. Men were not supposed to cry, especially not fathers. "Yuck," Jinx mouthed at me, her round white face like a horrified little moon in the shadows. I felt my own heart drop to my feet in a long, sickening fall. The next day, we were a lot nicer to Buddy on the beach.

Our mothers played bridge and went on a gin-and-tonic

diet, which meant that they walked up and down the beach a lot with insulated plastic tumblers in their hands. Jinx and I won cheap jewelry by throwing softballs at stuffed cats in the amusement park, rode rented bikes, and drank some gin of our own with three girls from Durham, North Carolina, who had stolen it from their parents. We bleached our hair with lemon juice. We got real tan, and did not burn our eyelids. The weather was perfect every day except for the last one, which dawned rainy, and so we packed up and drove home early to surprise our daddies.

They would be at work, of course, when we got there. Mama dropped Jinx and her mother off first, then let me out at home and went on to the grocery store. I let myself in with the key and took my bag upstairs to my room, which looked *smaller* now, a baby's room. I put my bag on the bed and turned to the mirror and then stopped still, in shock—I almost failed to recognize myself! My bleached blond hair, grown out longer than it had ever been, curled all around my dark face, which looked different, too . . . thinner, not so babyish.

I raced outside and got my bike out of the garage and rode off to see Carroll Byrd. It was a drizzly, humid August day; I was covered by a fine mist of rain, like my own sweat, by the time I turned down her lane. I rode until I reached the hedge where I always hid my bike, then slipped behind the farthest boxwood, looking toward the house.

But I went no closer.

For there, parked right in front, was Daddy's car, the familiar big gray Oldsmobile with the AAA and Rotary Club stickers. Even from where I was, I could see his old canvas hat stuck under the back windshield.

I waited and waited. At first I thought, *Oh well, Daddy's her lawyer. This is a lawyer visit.* Then I stopped thinking anything, as gradually it came over me. I didn't move a muscle. I stayed behind that boxwood for one hour and forty minutes by my watch, and then dodged back to the hedge and got my bike and rode home. When I went to bed that night, after Mama's special supper and Daddy's big hello, my arms and legs ached and ached, as if I had run a race, or climbed a mountain.

NEVER RODE MY bike to Carroll Byrd's house again. But the horrible thing was that I didn't really blame Daddy. I could see why he would love her. For in a sense, Daddy was *like* her: a loner, an observer, an outsider . . . despite the fact that he'd been born and brought up in Lewisville, despite the fact that he was doing exactly what he was supposed to be doing and had been at it for decades.

Daddy had run the mill, Dale Industries, since he was only twenty-eight years old, when his own father killed himself.

One day I asked Daddy to tell me about this. We were down at the mill, in the very office where my grandfather had done it. It was after hours, and Daddy was trying to finish up some paperwork, at the same desk where his father had kept the gun in the bottom drawer. "Why?" I kept asking. "Why did Granddaddy shoot himself?"

But all Daddy would say was, "Oh, Jenny, there are pressures, circumstances, that you can't possibly understand at your age"—the kind of response that infuriated me. I went right out in front of the mill and broke the aerial off Daddy's car, then lied about it. I said it had been done by some kids in a blue van with Ohio tags. Daddy always underrated me. As a future novelist and student of the human soul, I knew a lot more than he thought I did. I was capable of understanding anything he had to tell me.

I alone understood that Daddy was a hero, a tragic figure. He stood six-foot-three and looked like Gregory Peck, with a rangy body, a prominent nose, dark thick hair, and sad gray eyes that seemed to see *everything*. Perhaps to make up for his father's lapses, Daddy was the most responsible man in the world. He worked harder than anybody I have ever seen, involving himself not only in the daily business of the mill but also in the lives of the families who had been working there for generations: tirelessly attending funerals, weddings, graduations, wakes. My mother rarely went with him to these events, as she had "better things" to do, and also found "those people" depressing. Daddy served on every board in town and belonged to every organization, or so it appeared to me.

He also took care of my mean old grandmother and my shy maiden aunt Chloë, who lived with her, visiting them nearly every day. Aunt Chloë had had polio, and leaned to the left as she walked. My grandmother Ernestine Dale enjoyed absolutely *nothing* as far as I could see, except television; Daddy had bought them the first set in town. Grandmother claimed to watch only the quiz shows, calling them "educational," but in fact she watched that television all the time. She had trained Aunt Chloë to hop up and turn it off the moment a visitor arrived on the porch; by the time Aunt Chloë had let the visitor into the parlor, my grandmother would be reading the *Upper Room* or the Bible.

Oh, she *acted* simpery-sweet, but she didn't fool me for a minute—she was a fake, an old bitch. I didn't like her and she didn't like me much either, complaining that I was a "tomboy" and a "roughneck," criticizing my nails, which I bit to the quick, and trying to convince me that I should like Charles Van Doren better than Elvis Presley. My grandmother was a fool! She wore big black dresses and smelled like Mentholatum. I used to put baby powder in her tapioca and rearrange everything on her night table whenever I went to her house, so she would think she was going crazy.

I felt sorry for Daddy. He had to take care of Grandmother's and Aunt Chloë's affairs as well as our own; he also had to shepherd his other sister, my silly aunt Judy (that's Judy Dale Tuttle Miller Hall), in and out of one crazy marriage after another, while back at home he had two daughters to raise and then *me* (the surprise). Daddy had his work cut out for him. He had a beautiful wife who required a lot of coddling and catering to, something I'd always assumed he enjoyed, but after my observations of Carroll Byrd, I realized that Mama was *too* soft, *too* sweet, too safe for Daddy, like one of those pink satin pillows on her huge unmade bed. A man could sink down in there and never get out.

Now I saw Daddy as stifled, smothered by all that pink. I saw him as a restless cowboy in Grandmother's parlor, as a hawk among knickknacks.

No wonder he loved Carroll Byrd.

I still loved her, too; and in a way, I felt, this love brought me closer to my father, though he didn't know it, of course. But I was trying to *stop*, out of loyalty to my mother and also because I knew that Carroll Byrd would never love me back. She'd never even know me. The affair would not last long—these things never did, I told myself.

Anyway, I was used to loving people who didn't love me back. After all, I'd been in love with Tom Burlington, my sister's husband, for years and years. Three years, to be exact, but it seemed like an eternity.

MY SISTER CAROLINE *did not deserve* Tom Burlington. I couldn't imagine how she had tricked him into marrying her in the first place. My grandmother always called Caroline a flibbertigibbet: and for once, I agreed with her. Caroline was simply too bouncy. She wore everybody out. Of course she was a cheerleader at St. Catherine's; of course she was "Most Popular" in the yearbook; of course she was president of her class twice in a row at Hollins before transferring to Carolina in her junior year, where of course she pledged Tri Delt. She made solid B's and majored in elementary education. Caroline had a bouncy ponytail, boundless enthusiasm, and the whitest teeth I've ever seen. By Christmas of her senior year, she was engaged to Tom; right after graduation, they got married.

Caroline's wedding was the biggest event in our family that I could remember. My oldest sister, Beth, had married quietly (in the Little Chapel of St. Michael's Episcopal Church) before moving to California, where her young husband had gotten a very good job in the computer industry, which nobody had ever heard of. She had one child already, and was expecting another. I didn't know Beth at all, though I'd always felt that I'd *like* her, because of the sweet way she held her baby in the photographs she sent home. And when she and her husband came east for Caroline's wedding, Beth was the only person thoughtful enough to bring *me* a present: a silver ring with a turquoise flower. (I cried and cried when I lost it in the lake at Camp Nantahala the following summer.)

I was the youngest bridesmaid in Caroline's wedding. I got to wear a white organdy dress with a pink satin sash, a picture hat, and pearl earrings. I got to carry a bouquet of pink rosebuds and baby's breath. I even got to wear Cuban heels—my first high heels ever—over my grandmother's objections. She said I was too young. My mother said, "Oh, Ernestine, I'm sure you're right," and let me wear them anyway. I looked perfectly beautiful at Caroline's wedding, much prettier than Caroline herself, who was a bit too wholesome for white. Caroline looked like a nurse.

But her groom, Thomas Burlington, looked like Troy Donahue. He was the handsomest boy I'd ever met, and the nicest, possessing all of Daddy's sensitivity without the aloofness.

I had been predisposed toward him anyway, after Mama's discussions about him on the telephone: "Well, he doesn't have a penny to his name, but he's real *smart*, he's gotten all these scholarships. . . . Oh yes, we like him. You can't help but like him. . . . He's got a master's degree in English literature, have you *ever*? . . . Well I don't know. Teach school, I reckon." Mama's tone betrayed what she thought about teach-

ing school, and I was sure Caroline held the same opinion. A
schoolteacher would never be able to support Caroline, not
even the cutest schoolteacher in the world, which Tom was.
He didn't know what he was getting into. (Though they did
receive so many wedding presents that they could have sold
them off and lived for a year or two on the proceeds, it looked
like to me.)

The wedding reception was held at our house, under a huge
white tent set up in the backyard. In the house, the wedding
presents were displayed in the family room and the downstairs
guest suite, a sea of silver, china, and crystal. I had earlier
pocketed a nifty jade paperweight sent by one of Tom's rela-
tives that nobody had ever heard of, to keep as a souvenir.

I started loving Tom Burlington at the wedding reception,
and never stopped. The party was all but over. Tom and Caroline had cut the cake, made the toasts, and everybody was
dancing to terrible music (Percy Faith). Caroline had gone upstairs to put on her "going-away outfit." My feet were killing
me. I shifted from foot to foot to keep my heels from sinking
into the grass as I waited in the front yard, clutching my net
package of rice, wishing I hadn't gotten so grown up all of a
sudden, so I could run down the road playing tag with my
little cousins.

"Why don't you just take them off?" There was Tom at my
elbow. He pointed to my shoes.

"Oh, I'm fine," I said. "Just fine. I wear heels all the time,"
I said.

"I was just thinking of taking my own shoes off," Tom said. "In fact, I believe I will." He stepped out of his loafers and leaned down to peel off his socks. He had changed to a seersucker suit with a white shirt and a striped tie.

"Me too, then." My feet sank into the cool thick grass.

"And now, Miss Jennifer, I wonder if you would do me the honor of accompanying me to get another bite of that cake," Tom said formally. "There's plenty of time. You know how long it takes your sister to get dressed."

He held his arm out to me the way people do in movies, and I took it. We walked off, leaving our shoes where they were, and went over to the huge delicious complicated cake on its own table, attended by a waiter. "Which layer, Miss?" the waiter asked, and I said, "Chocolate, please." There was a white layer, a yellow layer, and a chocolate layer. Trust Caroline to have a fancier cake than anybody in Lewisville had ever had before.

Tom chose chocolate, too. "Now how about a drink?" he asked.

"I'd love some champagne," I said.

Tom didn't bat an eye. He disappeared and came right back with a glass of champagne for me and one for himself. He clinked my glass in an elegant toast: "To the lovely Miss Jennifer." This is the exact moment I fell in love. Then he quoted a real poem, which began: "A sweet disorder in the dress . . ." It was very long and very beautiful.

I held my breath the whole time. At the end of the poem, I

raised my glass and drained it. The champagne went straight up my nose. I started crying, and couldn't stop.

Tom was not at all disconcerted by my tears. He did not say "Don't cry" or "There now." Instead, he wiped at them gravely, scientifically, with a linen napkin. Then he took my arm again and escorted me gallantly across the grass to the front yard, where the whole crowd had gathered, with Mama up on the steps in her billowing satin gown, her hand to her forehead like an explorer, anxiously scanning the crowd.

"*Here* he is!" she called inside. "Okay, dear!" And then Caroline emerged in a beige suit with a corsage, carrying her bouquet. Before I knew it, Tom had moved to her side, and flashbulbs were popping, and then she threw the bouquet straight to me. Everybody cheered. I clutched it tight, forgetting to throw my own rice, while Tom and Caroline ran the gauntlet out to their waiting limo and rushed away to the Mountain Lake Hotel, where they would *do it* all night long. (Do *what*? I had no idea.) I saved that bouquet, though. I have it still.

When the wedding pictures came, everybody was amused to see that Tom had gone off on his honeymoon *barefooted.* Nobody but me knew why. Nobody but me ever knew that he had toasted me with champagne, and said a poem to me.

From that day forward, I loved Tom with a rapt, fierce, patient love. Sometimes I even talked myself into believing, for an hour or so at least, that Tom had married Caroline only to get closer to *me*, to wait for me to grow up. Other times, even I had to admit that their marriage seemed to be going okay.

Tom got a job teaching English at a boys' boarding school outside Charlottesville, which afforded them a nice free bungalow on campus, which Caroline immediately fixed up like a doll-house version of Mama's house. Tom got a promotion, then another promotion and a raise. Caroline taught second grade and joined the Junior League and gave little dinner parties using all her wedding presents. When Mama and I drove up for a Saturday visit, Caroline served us shrimp salad on bone china plates with a scalloped gold edge. She told us that she and Tom were very happy, which I had no reason to doubt.

Yet unrequited love is the easiest sort of love to hang on to, and I'd cherished mine for three years now, until it had become not only a passion but a habit. Whenever I heard Debbie Reynolds's hit recording of "Tammy," for instance, I'd change the words to "Tommy" in my mind:

The old hootie-owl
Hootie-hoos to the dove,
Tommy, Tommy,
Tommy's in love . . .

with *me*! His bare feet in the wedding pictures provided all the proof I needed. Of course I also liked the wedding pictures because I was in them, looking terrific.

However, I hated looking at Mama and Daddy's wedding pictures because I was *not* in them, because I hadn't even existed then, a fact which threw me into as much terror as the thought of my own death. I had tried to explain this to Jinx, but she didn't get it. Nobody got it.

I saw myself as an island with time stretching out before me and behind me, all around me like a deep lake, mysterious and never-ending, like Lake Nantahala, where I lost my ring, where a person might lose anything. This precarious view made everything that happened to me seem very, very important. I had to see as much as I could see, learn as much as I could learn, feel as much as I could feel. I had to live like crazy all the time, an attitude that would get me into lots of trouble later. So it didn't matter, not really, whether or not Tom loved me back. Sometimes—I knew this from observing Mama and her baby brother, Mason—you're bound to love most the one who loves you least, and least deserves it.

MASON WAS JUST no good. Everybody knew it, since he had come to live with Mama and Daddy when his parents—my grandparents—died unexpectedly in the same year, many years ago. Seventeen years older than I, Mason was grown and gone by the time I was born. He had graduated from our local high school by the skin of his teeth, distinguished by nothing—no sports, no clubs. Nice girls would not date him. College was out of the question. Mason wore T-shirts and the same old leather jacket all through high school; his swept-back hair was long and greasy. Even Daddy could not get a button-down shirt or a sports jacket on him.

Mason had been a *juvenile delinquent*. This thrilled me. Of course, I would have adored him if he'd been nice to me at all, but his interest in me was confined to ruffling my hair at infrequent intervals throughout my childhood and mumbling "Hey now" out of the side of his mouth. That was *it*. And now, after some awful fight, he and Daddy had had a "parting of the ways," as Mama put it. Daddy was a man who stood on principle, though the rift broke Mama's heart. I wasn't sure what the final straw had been. I knew that Daddy had bailed Mason out of debt numerous times and had set him up in two businesses, which had, however, failed. Somewhere along the way, Mason had married "disastrously," Mama said, a much older woman of no consequence, with three children. Her name was Gloria, but I had never met her, or even laid eyes on her. I hardly ever laid eyes on Mason, either. He lived someplace near Norfolk and worked in the shipyards, I think. He no longer showed up for holidays, and had not attended Caroline's wedding.

So by the time of this story, a sighting of Mason was as rare as a comet, taking place only during the daytime when Daddy was not at home. On those few occasions, Mason scared me a little—he'd grown fat and scruffy, and needed a shave. He didn't look like a juvenile delinquent anymore but like some guy you'd see on the side of a road hitchhiking. He looked older than he was, down on his luck.

Daddy was still officially waiting for Mason to "come around." In the meantime, Mama gave him money. That's what these visits were all about: money. I knew it, though Mama never said so. She received Mason privately—in her bedroom or the Florida room or the living room—anywhere I was *not*, which she made sure of by closing whatever door existed between me and them. When Mason left, looking shifty, Mama always seemed to have her purse nearby—on her bed, or the coffee table, or the sofa. Wherever they'd just been. I could put two and two together. She didn't have to tell me not to tell Daddy, either; I already knew that. Just as I knew that Mason never came to see her unless he needed money, and this must have hurt her deeply.

Mama always had a good cry the minute he left. "Oh, Jenny, honey, come here and hug your mama," she'd call, and I would go do it, patting her plump shoulder ineffectively while she sobbed into her pink Kleenex. "That poor soul," she'd wail, "that poor, poor soul!"

I didn't even like Mason by then, and couldn't understand why Mama would waste her tears on him when she had such a brilliant and adorable daughter right there on the premises. Now, so many years later and a parent myself, I understand that there is no anguish like the anguish of not being able to make a loved one become the person you think he ought to be. It can't be done, of course. But they had not given up on him yet, not Mama and not even Daddy. Why, Mason was barely thirty years old! Surely he'd come to his senses. Surely he'd shape up.

In the fall of 1958, Mama and Daddy were still expecting this to happen.

JINX AND I were in my room listening to records when the call came. It was a Saturday afternoon, bright and blowing outside, leaves flying everyplace. We lay stretched out flat on the shag carpet trying to figure out what in the world "*Nel blu, dipinto di blu*" meant, and sighing over "Fever" by Peggy Lee. We knew what that meant. I had just put "Love Me Tender" on when the phone rang. Jinx jumped up. She was hoping to hear from Stevie Burns, who had said he'd call her this weekend; I knew Jinx had made her mother promise to give him our number before she'd agree to come over to my house at all. Since summer, Jinx had, one, started her period and, two, gotten popular, just like that. She wouldn't go spying with me anymore.

I had a phone in my room, and Jinx grabbed it on the first ring. "Hello," she said. Her new poodle cut gave her a heart-shaped face, eager now.

I sat up, too, vicariously excited, thinking I might pick up some useful pointers for handling future dates. So I was watching closely as Jinx's smiling mouth went into that frozen O, as she shut her brown eyes for a long moment before carefully replacing the receiver on its cradle.

Downstairs, Mama started to scream.

"Oh, Jenny." Jinx finally spoke. "Your uncle is dead."

"What?" I had to think for a moment to figure out who she was talking about.

"Mason," she said. "Isn't his name Mason? Mason's been shot."

"Shot," I repeated.

"Murdered," Jinx said.

The word hung in the air in my bedroom, quivering along with Elvis's voice. I turned the record player off just as Mama rushed through the bedroom door, swooping me up, smothering me with her sobs and tears.

The story, what we could learn of it, went like a country song. Mason's wife had left him for another man, and Mason had gone out looking for her. He'd found them at last in some bar in Norfolk, where things had turned ugly fast. Mason had pulled a knife and cut the man's face. Then the man shot him.

"Shot him dead?" I asked Mama.

"No, honey. Shot him *four times* before he died." Mama collapsed on my canopied bed, wailing. "He was the most adorable little boy," she cried. "I was just a newlywed myself when he came to live with us, you know. Just a girl. Your daddy was always working, always gone. So it was just Mason and me. We grew up together. He was the sweetest boy, you can't imagine. Maybe he was *too* sweet, maybe that was the problem, he just never could get along. And then all that drinking, oh Lord, it started so soon. If only—if only we—" Mama went on and on.

Jinx sneaked out, looking panicked. She waved from the door. I sat on the side of my bed hugging Mama for what seemed like hours, until Jinx's mother arrived. I was never so glad to see anybody in my life. Then suddenly my wild aunt Judy was there, too, serious for once; and our minister, Mr. Clyde Vereen; and then Dr. Nevins, who gave Mama some pills which shut her up all right but made her *too calm*, I felt.

Mama sat downstairs on a tufted velvet love seat, where she had never sat before, at least not in my memory, vacant and glassy-eyed, asking for Daddy. Meanwhile, Aunt Judy was on the phone constantly, and Jinx's mama answered the door.

"Where is John?" Mama kept asking. "I just can't understand where John is."

Nobody else could understand this, either. Aunt Judy couldn't reach him out at Granddaddy's old hunting cabin, where Daddy had gone for the night. He did this occasionally, though he'd read and reflect instead of hunt. It was his retreat.

Finally Aunt Judy dispatched his good friend George Long to get him, but an hour and a half later George called back with the perplexing message that Daddy was not at the hunting cabin, and it didn't look like he'd even gotten there yet. Our house was filling up with people and food; I was amazed at how fast the news spread. Jinx came back over to "be with me." It was not until I saw her in her church dress that I realized the seriousness of what had happened.

The phone kept ringing and people kept coming in and going out. Arrangements were made. They were sending Mason's body over from Norfolk in a hearse. It would arrive at our local funeral home by evening. Mr. Joines, the undertaker, came in. He talked to Mama, who did not seem to understand what he was saying. She smiled and smiled, in a way that scared me. My grandmother arrived, all dressed up, and started bossing everybody around.

There was so much going on that I barely registered the arrival of Mr. Kinney, Daddy's foreman and "right hand man" from the mill, still in his work clothes, holding his hat in his hands. Mr. Kinney went straight to my aunt Judy and took her aside for a whispered conference, then left without speaking to Mama or me. He ducked his head as he went out the door. And the afternoon wore on, the longest day I had ever lived through, the longest day in the world.

It was almost night when Daddy finally came home. Jinx and I were sitting in the window seat in the living room, balancing plates of ham sandwiches and potato salad on our knees, when a red car pulled up and stopped at the end of our walk. I thought I had seen the car before, but I couldn't remember where. I peered out through the gathering dark. Daddy got out on the passenger side of the car and then I could see him plain in the light at the end of our walk. He looked years older than he had the day before.

Daddy stared out at our house, then opened the door and leaned down into the car to say something. He straightened up and looked at the house again. The other door of the car opened and Carroll Byrd got out, wearing pants, her hair streaming down her back. She walked around the front of the car to Daddy, who put out his arms and held her for a long time, so long I couldn't believe it.

Didn't he *know* that this house was full of people who could look out the windows and see him, and see what he was doing? Didn't he *care*? Didn't he even care at all about Mama, or me, or anybody except himself?

Finally, Carroll Byrd stepped away from Daddy, who touched her cheek once and then turned and came slowly up the walk, as if to his own execution. Carroll Byrd got back in her car and drove away, and I never saw her again.

The funeral was held two days later at St. Michael's Episcopal Church, though Mason had not been there or to any other church for many years, as far as we knew. The funeral church was packed anyway, with Mama and Daddy's friends and lots of people from the mill. Mason's wife did not show up, but two of her daughters did, trashy girls in their late teens with curly red hair who cried like they meant it and told Mama that Mason had been a great stepfather to them. I know this was more important to Mama than anything else that was said at Mason's funeral. She clung to their arms, and gave them money later.

My oldest sister Beth could not come for the funeral, as

she was nearing the end of a difficult pregnancy, but Caroline came, of course, with Tom—my beloved Tom, who immediately made himself indispensable to everybody, with his good sense and calm, reasonable manner.

After the funeral, Tom and Grandmother stood by the door and shook hands and talked to everybody who came to our house, while Mama and Caroline sat together on the love seat and cried. They looked like beautiful strangers to me—the big disheveled blonde, the pretty girl with mascara streaking her face. My old terror came back as I realized I didn't have a clue as to what their family had been like, how they had acted with each other, who they were before I was born. I got the same feeling in my stomach that I'd had at the beach when Jinx and I spied on Mr. Womble. Daddy talked on the telephone back in his study with the door closed, though Aunt Judy tried several times to get him to come out and "act responsible." (Imagine *Aunt Judy* saying this to *Daddy*!)

At length Grandmother left her post in the front hall and walked to Daddy's study, magisterial in her black suit. I followed, slipping into the stairwell. I understood that Grandmother had been dressing for a funeral for years, and now was in her element. Grandmother went into the study and shut the door behind her. I am not sure what she said to Daddy, but it all ended with her marching out and him shouting, "God damn it, Mama!" and slamming the door.

"But John!" Grandmother had apparently thought of something else to say. She turned and tried the knob. He had locked the door. She was furious, I knew, but when she saw me, her face fell into its customary haughty expression, and she sailed into the living room without another word, to shake hands and smile some more.

I headed to the kitchen for a Coke, and there I discovered Aunt Judy in the process of getting drunk. She'd done absolutely as much as she *could*, Goddamnit! she said. Now it was out of her hands entirely. Nobody could blame her.

It seemed to be out of *everyone's* hands.

I got back to the living room just in time to hear Caroline announce her own pregnancy. Tom stood beside her, straight as a soldier, grinning from ear to ear, the bastard. I felt like I'd been kicked in the stomach.

"Oh, John," Mama began calling. "Oh, John!" She blew her nose on her pink Kleenex. "Oh, John, come here, darling, we've got some *good* news after all, even on this awful day! Oh, John . . ." she kept calling, but Daddy never came.

I spent the night at Jinx's. Locked in the bathroom, we smoked a whole pack of her mother's Kents, which tasted awful. Then I slept for twelve hours solid. I awoke to find both Jinx and her mother sitting on the end of Jinx's extra twin bed staring fixedly at me.

"Oh, thank goodness," Jinx's mother said in a fuzzy, distracted way, which was not like her at all. "Oh, Jenny, honey."

I could tell that she knew everything, all about Daddy and Carroll Byrd, which probably meant that everybody else knew everything, too. What a big relief! I didn't realize how hard it had been to keep such a secret until I felt the weight of it leave me like a physical thing, like a rock being lifted off the top of my head. For the first time in months, I could cry—and I did. I cried and cried and cried, for Mama and Daddy and Carroll Byrd and poor terrible scary dead Mason, who had been the sweetest child, and for myself and especially for the loss of Tom Burlington, who would never be free to love me now.

THIS IS WHERE everything gets all hazy in my mind. By the time I went home from Jinx's, Daddy was gone. I did not have to be told where he was. I knew he was with her. Mama was brightly, determinedly cheerful, wearing that same crazy smile which had scared me so much before. She was in the kitchen cooking up a storm, banging the pots around, while Dot, our maid, watched her anxiously.

"Oh, hello, dear," Mama said to me. "I'm making some potato soup, I think potato soup is just so *comforting*, and Lord knows, we can all use a little comfort, isn't that right, Dot?"

"Yes ma'am," Dot said.

Mama wore a green knit suit with lots of gold jewelry, including her famous charm bracelet. I looked to see if Daddy's Deke pin was still on it. It was.

"Jenny," she said brightly to me, stirring. "Did you hear that your daddy has had to go out of town on an extended business trip? He said to give you his love and tell you he'll be back before long. I made this potato soup for you, honey," she added. "I know it's your favorite."

It was the first time in my life that I had ever been unable to eat. Mama didn't even try. She just sat across from me drumming her beautiful red nails on the table, rat-a-tat-tat, and sipping from a tall Kentucky Derby glass.

I thought she had water in the glass, but it was vodka, and she filled it again as soon as the level dipped below half, and did not put it down for the next two weeks. She never quit talking, either, to me or Dot or Jinx's mother or one or another of her friends. They had arranged it among themselves so that someone was always with her, and every day when I came home from school, there they'd be, Mama and her visitor (Buffy, Bitsy, Helen, Jane Ann, etc.), talking a mile a minute with Dot hovering in the background. Mama kept cooking those nice little suppers for me, which we never ate. Dinnertime was my time to entertain her, though, while Dot and Mama's friends went home to their own families, before Aunt Judy showed up to spend the night.

Mostly we read movie magazines and talked about the lives of the stars. So much had happened lately that we had a lot to catch up on. Judy Garland was divorcing Sid Luft, and that "ideal couple," Cary Grant and Betsy Drake, had parted, amicably though. Jean Seberg was engaged to some Frenchman she'd met in the romantic resort town of Saint-Tropez, on the French Riviera, while she was filming *Bonjour Tristesse*. Tyrone Power married Debbie Minardos in a little chapel in her hometown of Tunica, Mississippi.

We were still reveling in Grace Kelly's fairy-tale wedding to Prince Rainier, and in the Robert Wagner–Natalie Wood marriage. We could tell that Janet Leigh and Tony Curtis were truly in love; Mama explained to me that their union had brought Tony (born Bernard Schwartz) "up into a better class of people." And Kim Novak was dating Sammy Davis, Jr., which outraged Mama. I didn't care. I thought Kim Novak was beautiful, and planned to paint my entire room lavender, just like hers, whenever Mama would let me.

I still could not understand how the gorgeous Marilyn Monroe could have married such a dried-up pruny old guy as Arthur Miller, though Mama said he was a brilliant egghead intellectual. "They have their charms," she told me, sipping from her glass, ignoring the fried chicken she had just cooked.

This was as close as Mama ever came to mentioning Daddy.

After supper we watched television together, an unaccustomed treat since Daddy didn't like for the television set to be on in the evenings except for *Huntley–Brinkley* or an occasional dramatic production. But now Mama and I watched everything, and she kept up a running commentary. Her favorites were the variety shows, where she could see the most stars. I thought *Ed Sullivan* and *Your Hit Parade* were okay, but I personally liked the Dinah Shore show the best, especially the end, where she sang "See the *U.S.A.* in your *Chev*rolet," and blew a big, smacking kiss to the studio audience. Mama invariably turned to me at this point and whispered, "Of course, you know Dinah has Negro blood."

"How do you know that?" I'd asked the first couple of times Mama said this, but all she ever answered was, "Oh, honey, *everybody* knows it!" Whether everybody did or not, Mama believed it implicitly, as she believed in flying saucers and reincarnation and segregation and linen napkins and Chanel No. 5 and not going swimming for one hour after eating and not having milk with fish.

Mama and I watched television together until about nine o'clock, when Aunt Judy would show up to give Mama her pills and I'd be free to do my homework or go to bed and read for as long as I liked. I was reading *By Love Possessed* (pretty hot stuff), which had just arrived in a package from the Book-of-the-Month Club. I kept it under my bed.

We went on this way for about three weeks, until that awful night when we were watching *What's My Line?* together. Now, I really liked *What's My Line?* I felt that its question-and-answer format offered some good pointers for a combination spy and novelist such as myself. First "the challenger" would come into the studio and sign in on the blackboard. The challenger could be a man or a woman, either one. Then words would flash up on the screen, telling the audience what the challenger did for a living. The job was always far out—one man polished jelly beans, another put sticks in Popsicles, another was a bull de-horner. I loved these jobs, which made me feel that the world was a much more open place than I had been led to believe thus far. It was clear that I was destined to go to St. Catherine's and make my debut, but after college, who knows? I imagined going on the show myself someday as the challenger, the youngest best-selling author in the world.

Anyway, the panelists asked questions to figure out the challenger's line, such as:

"Are you self-employed?"

"Do you deal in services?"

"Do people come to you? Men and women both?"

"Are they happier when they leave?"

"Do you need a college education to do what you do?"

I imagined Carroll Byrd as the challenger, squirming while she tried to answer this question, cringing when Dorothy Kilgallen pointed a finger at her and cried: "You are an *adulteress*!"

On the night I am thinking about, the challenger was a professional fire-eater and the panel was closing in. "Oh, he'll get it now," I said to Mama, because it was Bennett Cerf's turn and he was the smartest. "Don't you think? Hmmm? Don't you think?"

When Mama didn't answer, I turned and saw that she had slumped over to one side in the easy chair, her head too far down on her shoulder, exactly like a bird with a broken neck. Her overturned drink made a spreading stain on her silk print dress. I watched while the Kentucky Derby glass rolled slowly off her lap and onto the carpet and under the coffee table. Then I got up and went to the telephone to call Aunt Judy, who didn't answer. I let it ring and ring. Finally I realized: Aunt Judy was already on her way. I stood by the front door, not moving, until she got there.

OTS OF THINGS happened immediately after that. Daddy appeared and took Mama out of the local hospital and drove her to a "lovely place" in Asheville, North Carolina, for a "nice little rest." I wouldn't even speak to him. I stayed in my room smoking cigarettes until they left. Then I had a big fight with my grandmother, refusing to stay with her and Aunt Chloë, claiming I'd rather be dead and would kill myself with a knife if they tried to make me. Nobody knew what to do. I had become a "problem child." I hoped to say with Jinx, of course, but Jinx's mother announced unexpectedly that she thought this would not be a good idea just now, that Jinx and I were "not good influences" on each other. And furthermore Aunt Judy had "*had* it" with all of us, she said, and was off to Bermuda for a much-needed vacation. So I stayed at our house and Dot stayed in the guest room until Daddy came back and got me and took me down to visit Mama's cousins in Repass, South Carolina, where I had never been. I wouldn't go until Mama begged me on the phone, and then I had to. I had to do anything she wanted me to do. My mother's cousin was named Glenda. They were sending me to her because she was a school principal whose home had "structure," which I "needed," and because she had a daughter about my age, who was a "model girl" and would be my friend.

I doubted this, and didn't speak to Daddy the entire way down to South Carolina in the car, though he tried and tried to talk to me and never lost his patience, not even when he saw me spit in his Coke at a Howard Johnson's. He looked at me sadly, solemnly, like a tragic hero. Daddy had dark circles beneath his eyes now, and his hands shook. He was supposedly living for love, but it seemed to me more like he was dying of it. I hated him. I hated him for being so weak, for loving her more than he loved us. I also hated Mama—for letting this happen, for getting sick, for going to the hospital. For abandoning me. I hated Aunt Judy for going to Bermuda, and my sisters for being so involved with their own jobs and babies and lives. I hated Jinx because she got to stay with her own happy family while I had to go live with complete strangers in South Carolina.

I already hated everybody I knew, so I was prepared to hate cousin Glenda on sight. And what a sight she was! Though I was told I had met her before, when I was little, I couldn't remember . . . and surely I would have remembered anybody as awful as this. Cousin Glenda looked like a fireplug, or maybe a built-in barbecue grill. She was five-by-five, and wore an orange suit with a flowered blouse and brown lace-up shoes when I first saw her. They were the ugliest shoes in the world. Her hair was a bright yellow lacquered helmet squished way down on her head. It was impossible for me to believe that she was related to Mama, or that they had grown up together. I had heard Mama say that she and Glenda "did not always see eye to eye" on things. Now I understood this was a huge understatement. Cousin Glenda was as hard as Mama was soft, as practical as she was flighty, as ugly as she was pretty, as mean as she was sweet.

Cousin Glenda stood in the driveway with her arms crossed and her feet planted wide apart as we drove up. Behind her, their house was completely square, as square as she was, as if it were made out of building blocks. It was a plain two-story brick house with no shutters and no shrubbery, sitting smack in the middle of a square green yard, with a walk going up to the front door and a maple tree planted on each side.

"I don't want to stay here." It was the first thing I had said all day.

Daddy turned off the car. "Honey, it's only for a little while. You know that. It's just until your mama gets out of the hospital."

"I can't stay here," I said.

"Honey, please."

It occurred to me that *Daddy* might cry.

"Let's get your things out," he said. "This won't be for long, I promise."

"*Sure*." I sounded every bit as sarcastic as Buddy Womble.

Cousin Glenda rolled toward us like a tank. "I'll take that," she said to Daddy, grabbing my suitcase. "Come on now, Jennifer," she said to me, and I surprised myself by getting out of the car. She grabbed my elbow. Her grip was iron. "Okay, John, I'll take care of her. Send a check every week, and call her every Sunday night. That's it, then."

Cousin Glenda was talking *at* my father instead of *to* him, as if he were some lower order of being, and suddenly I felt my allegiance shifting in an alarming about-face, back toward Daddy. I felt that I could be as mean to him as I wanted to, as mean as he deserved, but I couldn't stand for anybody else to be mean to him.

"Daddy, Daddy, Daddy," I said, and he stepped over to me quickly and gave me a tight, fierce hug. "It'll be all right, Jenny. It will. It won't be long, you'll see." Close up, Daddy smelled like cigarettes and Aqua Velva, his old smell, and then I loved him more than anybody in the world and wanted to die for hating him so much and spying on him and spitting in his Coke at Howard Johnson's and for the many other awful things I'd done.

"Come along now, Jennifer." Cousin Glenda had a voice that made you do everything she said.

"You're hurting my arm." I tried to shake her off, but she held on like a bulldog.

"I know all about you, Miss," she announced with a great deal of satisfaction, pulling me toward the house. "We're going to put the quietus on you."

T HE QUIETUS! WHAT was *that*? I was terrified. But I soon learned that this was simply one of cousin Glenda's favorite sayings. She was always going to "put the quietus" on somebody, or telling somebody to "get a grip." She'd say, "Your mother called today, Jennifer, and said how much she hated doing all the things she has to do up there, such as exercise, and I said to her, 'Billie, get a grip!' I just hope she was taking it in."

Cousin Glenda quoted herself endlessly, infatuated with her own good advice. She'd say, "That new substitute teacher came in my office all upset because we had to cut fifteen minutes off of second period for the fire drill, and I said, 'Mr. Johnson, get a grip!'" Cousin Glenda reminded me of a blowfish, all puffed up and blustery, and I soon understood that I didn't really need to be afraid of her. She was all hot air and good intentions. Growing up as one of Mama's poor relations in Charleston, she had idolized Mama for her sweetness and generosity. Now that Mama was in trouble and had no brothers and sisters of her own, cousin Glenda was more than willing to step in and help her out. She would shape me up. She would *make* me get a grip. And for a fact, it was easier to get a grip in that household than in our own, where so many things were too slippery to hold on to and so many words were never spoken and the rules were always changing.

The rules in cousin Glenda's house were inflexible, and everybody toed the line. "Everybody" included her husband, Raymond, long-faced and lantern-jawed but clearly nice, who didn't have a chance to get a word in edgewise with cousin Glenda around, repeating word for word every conversation she'd ever had. I can't remember hearing Raymond speak once during the whole time I was there, though this can't be true. He grinned a lot, however, as if he got a big kick out of cousin Glenda—out of us all, in fact. Raymond would never leave *his* wife. They had been married since they were both eighteen, and he had worked at the same job in the post office for twenty-three years. He wasn't going *anywhere.*

Rayette, my model cousin, turned out to be a junior version of her mother. One year older than I, freckled, sturdy, and curly-haired, she had a wide plain face and big cornflower-blue eyes and not one ounce of irony or guile. I knew immediately that Rayette would never understand my spying, which I would never tell her about. I hid my Davy Crockett notebook under my mattress. Rayette was fascinated by me, and especially all my cool stuff: the red plastic case containing my 45-rpm records, my Tangee lipstick and fashionable clothes, especially the crinolines and my two appliquéd circle skirts; my castle-shaped jewelry box with its own lock and key, containing my add-a-pearl necklace and Captain Midnight decoder ring and jade paperweight and fourteen separate items (such as a ballpoint pen and a jujube wrapper) that had been touched by Tom Burlington. But Rayette did not have a jealous bone in her body. She seemed as glad to have me there as her parents were, and curiously enough, I did not mind being there, either, or obeying all the rules or following the rigid schedule.

I loved this schedule, which included getting up at the crack of dawn because we had to catch the school bus, saying the blessing and sitting down to eat a huge breakfast of eggs and bacon and grits, and then making our own beds and washing the dishes (no Dot) before we set out through the foggy chill of the lowland South Carolina morning to stand by the road and stamp our feet and blow out our breath in puffy clouds and wait for the big yellow school bus to come blasting out of the mist like an apparition and carry us away. Back home, Daddy or Dot had always driven me to school.

Rayette's school was a hick school, as Jinx had predicted it would be, but as the new girl, I was more popular than I had ever been, and reveled in this development. All the girls wanted to sit next to me at lunch. All the boys bumped into me in the hall, acting dumb. A's were easy to come by. After school, I'd stay late with Rayette for her 4-H and Tri-Hi-Y meetings—clubs I would have scorned back home. They were just beginning a sewing project in 4-H, and so I, too, got to make a terrible-looking bright yellow blouse with a scoop neck, and sleeves that did not fit the armholes, and darts in the wrong place. I was intensely proud of myself.

Rayette was president of Tri-Hi-Y, a Christian service club that pledged itself to goodness at every meeting and did good deeds all over the county. While I was there, they were raising money to buy an artificial leg for a little boy named Leonard Pipkin. Rayette called each meeting to order by banging on a table with a gavel. This gavel impressed me so much that I gave up espionage and literature on the spot, and vowed to be just like her. I wanted to bang on a table with my gavel, to run clubs, to wear a huge cross around my neck every day, a cross so big it would pitch me forward and weigh me down, and most of all, to be *absolutely sure* about everything in the world.

The main criterion in cousin Glenda's house was, "What would Jesus think of this?" Jesus did not think much of rock and roll, for instance. Specifically, He did not like fast records that caused young people to move their bodies in sinful ways. He hated "Whole Lot-ta Shakin' Goin' On," "Wake Up, Little Susie," and "Blue Suede Shoes," so these had to stay in my special case, but I was allowed to play "Que Será, Será," "April Love," and (strangely) "The Great Pretender." Jesus was very picky.

He apparently prized neatness, cleanliness, and order above all things; I imagined that the plastic runners on the living room carpet and the cellophane covers on all the lampshades were His idea. I liked them myself as they gave the living room such a weird, ghostly aspect, and the runners popped and crinkled nicely when you walked on them. Lots of things had covers in cousin Glenda's house—the toaster, the Mixmaster, and the blender wore matching piqué jackets with rickrack around the edges; the Kleenex box and the Jergens lotion bottle had crocheted skirts; the toilets featured big fuzzy pads.

And everything had its place. I learned this fast. Rayette burst into tears the third day I was there because I had borrowed her hairbrush (without asking) and put it back in the wrong place, and so it wasn't *exactly where it was supposed to be* when she needed it. Pearl Harbor! This threw Rayette for such a loop that I never did it again, striving for a Jesusy order as great as hers. I got into it. I put my shoes in a row in my closet, as if some dainty princess were going to step into them at any minute. I rolled my socks into balls. I learned where all the dishes went, and everything in the refrigerator. I loved to fill the bird feeder and put away the groceries, both tasks that had to be done just so.

Another virtue right up there with order was *being prepared.* "Jesus will look after you, honey," cousin Glenda often said, "but He expects you to do what you can." Therefore the family was prepared for any possible crisis, with a first-aid kit, emergency flares, a snakebite kit, a shotgun, and—wonder of wonders—a Bomb Shelter!

Rayette didn't appear to care too much about the Bomb Shelter one way or the other—I guess she was used to it—but I thought it was the coolest thing I had ever seen, the coolest

place I'd ever been. You went down into the Bomb Shelter
through a trap door in the garage. This was an orange metal
door with three black X's on it. It was impervious to radiation.
You had to go down a dozen steep steps into the cavelike Bomb
Shelter itself, which was equipped with all the necessities for
nuclear war, including:

> *A Geiger counter with its $98.50 price tag still attached*
> *A two-way portable radio*
> *A pick and shovel*
> *A chemical toilet (Rayette explained that you would put a*
> *   blanket over yourself, for privacy, when you used it.)*
> *Mattresses and blankets*
> *A Sterno stove*
> *A fire extinguisher*
> *Paper products*
> *Canned water*
> *Canned food and drinks*

It was always cold down there, and it was lit by a faint blue
light that buzzed with a thrillingly extraterrestrial sound. I
loved to sit in the Bomb Shelter. I also loved to survey the
backyard from the kitchen window while I washed dishes,
thinking, *The Bomb Shelter is right out there! Nobody knows it,
nobody can possibly tell, nobody knows it but us!* I spent as much
time in the Bomb Shelter as I could get away with, without at-

tracting too much attention to myself, whenever we weren't at school or doing chores or praying or going to church.

We went to church a lot. We went to church every time they cracked the door; but even at home, we'd pray at the drop of a hat. We prayed over everything: that I would make an A on my math test, that the lady up the street would see the light (what light?), that Mama would get well soon and Daddy would see the error of his ways and Jesus would forgive him, that the family's old station wagon would make it through the winter without a new clutch, that the upcoming Tri-Hi-Y bake sale would be a big success and Leonard Pipkin would get a new leg. Cousin Glenda would throw one hand up, bow her head, and set into praying whenever she felt like it, and then we'd all have to bow our heads and pray, too. Used to the sedate and abstract *Book of Common Prayer,* I was as startled by the personal nature of these prayers as by their frequency.

The church itself was even more unnerving. It was very plain, a cinder-block building that looked as if it might have once been a grocery store. There was nothing about it now to suggest that it was a church except for a hand-painted sign over the front door that read "Bible Church of God, All Enter In." I knew that "enter in" was redundant, like "Ford car," yet I found it mysteriously compelling, an invitation to a foreign country. And I was fascinated by what went on inside: clapping, singing, crying, hugging, and shouting amen—I had never seen any thing like it at St. Michael's, that's for sure.

"Bible" was the key to everything. "If it's not Bible, we don't believe in it, and we don't do it," cousin Glenda explained.

"But the Bible was written a long time ago," I pointed out. "Before airplanes or electricity or anything. How do you know Jesus wants you to have electricity?" I asked. "How do you know He wants you to have a phone? How do you know He doesn't like the Everly Brothers? How do you know He doesn't like eye makeup? There wasn't any makeup back in the Bible days, so—"

"Jennifer, Jennifer," cousin Glenda said, hugging me, "get a grip."

I tried to. I had given up spying entirely, except for one quick peep into Rayette's bedroom window to ascertain that, yes, she really did have breasts as big as softballs, obscured by the homemade shirtwaist dresses and shapeless blocky sweaters she always wore. I did not have the heart to spy on cousin Glenda and Raymond, however. The prospect of either one of them actually taking off their clothes was too awful to contemplate, much less their *doing it*. (What was *it*? I still didn't know.) But I was sure they had done it only once, whatever it was, in order to conceive Rayette and populate the earth.

Rayette (big as a woman, dumb as a post) soon became my personal servant and bodyguard. She carried my books to school, ironed my clothes, and once even hemmed a skirt for me. Cousin Glenda shook her head at this, smiling. "That's exactly how I was with your mama," she said. "Just exactly. I was three years younger than Billie, and if Billie said 'Jump!'

I said 'How far?' I used to follow her around everyplace, but if I got on her nerves she never let on, at least she never let on to me."

"What was Mama like, as a little girl?" I asked. I couldn't imagine this.

"An angel," my tough cousin Glenda answered immediately. "Oh, Jennifer, she was an angel."

I was no angel, but I was *trying*—trying not to spy, trying to get a grip, trying to be good. Now that I realized how good it was possible to be, I realized how bad I'd always been; and I got the idea that it was all my fault somehow, everything that had happened, and that if I could just be *good enough*, Mama and Daddy might get back together. So I was almost killing myself being as good as I could possibly be, which did not come naturally to me; but before long, sure enough, it worked.

One Sunday, Daddy reported that he had good news, that Mama was improving, and that we might all take a vacation together when she got out of the hospital. He did not mention Carroll Byrd. I was elated. I knew I had done this by being so good. I doubled my efforts, making three dozen brownies to sell at the Tri-Hi-Y bake sale to buy Leonard Pipkin that new leg.

There was a boy in the Tri-Hi-Y club who liked me, and I sort of knew it, though we had not exchanged two words. His name was Harlan Boyd. Everybody knew who he was because he was a big deal, the star football player. A *jock*. His neck was as thick as his head, which made his head and his neck together look like one single unit, like a fencepost topped off by his fuzzy brown flat-top. He had square jock shoulders and wore his red satin letter jacket all the time, with blue jeans. (Nobody cool wore blue jeans yet, this was before they got popular. Then, in Repass, blue jeans meant you were poor.) Harlan Boyd was in Rayette's grade, though he was in my math class. He was big for his age, and came from a "troubled home." He lived someplace out in the swamp with his uncle, under conditions too awful to imagine, yet he could catch a football like a dream and run like hell. These skills would be his ticket out of there, but he didn't know it yet, had not thought that far ahead. In fact, he probably hadn't thought much about anything yet, at age fifteen, that day at the bake sale.

The sale was held downtown in front of the courthouse, in the center of Repass, one Saturday in early December. Cousin Glenda, the Tri-Hi-Y sponsor, brought two card tables from home in the station wagon. Rayette rode over with her, and they were just getting everything set up when I arrived. Though I was trying my dead-level best to be good, I did not really like to be identified with cousin Glenda in public situations and so had turned down her offer of a ride and walked to the square by myself, bearing my platter of brownies. I hung back behind the giant live-oak tree, while cousin Glenda, wearing the world's largest car coat, bossed everybody around.

"Susan, put that right there!" she barked. "Rayette, pull

the tablecloth down! Peter, go get some change from the Rex-all!" Cousin Glenda was a world-class expert on bake sales, as on everything. Rayette, too innocent to know she ought to be embarrassed, did everything her mother told her, smiling placidly. (Oh, *she* was the angel, not me; I could never be that good!) I stayed hidden where I was until everything had been set up to cousin Glenda's satisfaction.

"All right now, boys and girls," she announced in a voice like a trumpet, raising her arm, "let us join hands and pray together, and ask our Heavenly Father to bless this bake sale and all this good food and all the proceeds therefrom, and may Leonard Pipkin get his new leg a.s.a.p., amen."

Looking sheepish, all the kids dropped one another's hands like hot potatoes while cousin Glenda stomped off to her station wagon for a cigarette (Jesus did not mind for adults to smoke), and I sallied forth with my brownies.

I'm still not sure how it happened. All I know is that one minute I was holding the brownies out in front of me like a sacrificial offering, and the next minute they were flying through the air like miniature UFOs and I was pitching forward, forward, forward in horrible slow motion forever, until I slammed into the wide solid chest of Harlan Boyd, propelling him backward, overturning one of the card tables and sending pound cakes and homemade bread and fudge everywhere. It was awful. It was the most awful and embarrassing thing I had done in my life up to that point, and it ended at last with me and Harlan Boyd splayed out on the ground against the card table, my cheek smashed into the letters on his football jacket, RR for Repass Rattlers. The letters felt scratchy and wonderful against my cheek. I could hear my own heart beating in my ears, so loud I thought briefly I might be having a heart attack.

"Jennifer, Jennifer, Jennifer!" squealed Rayette. "Are you okay?"

Then cousin Glenda was there too, pulling us up, brushing us off, getting everything to rights. I wanted to die, of course. I stood to the side with Rayette cooing over me, and would not even look at Harlan Boyd, who kept trying to say something to me. I had gotten pink icing on my blouse and mud on my crinoline, which hung way down below my skirt so everyone could see. Cousin Glenda drove me home to change. I told her I'd walk right back, though I had no intention of going back, *ever*, or of ever speaking to any of those kids again, especially not to Harlan Boyd, whose athletic letters had made a red mark like a rope burn on my cheek.

After I showered I kept touching it, looking at my face in the mirror. I put on some clean slacks and a sweater, but I couldn't find it in me to start back over to the bake sale. Instead I wandered around the still, sunny house. It was the first time I had been there alone, and it put me in mind of home, where I had often been the only child and had had the run of the house, and had done whatever I wanted. I started feeling spacy, detached from myself, between things.

The doorbell rang.

I opened it to find Harlan, letter jacket and all, there on the stoop. Though red-faced, he spoke up bravely: "I just wanted to see how you was," he said.

"I'm okay," I told him. "Come on in." I grabbed his sleeve and pulled him inside the house quickly, and shut the door. Now that I had him inside, however, I had no idea what to do with him. "My name is Jenny," I said stupidly.

"I know that," Harlan said. "You're not from around here, are you?"

"No," I said. "I'm just staying with my cousins until my parents get out of the hospital. They were in a train wreck," I added.

"Aw, shoot," Harlan said. "That's awful. Are they going to be okay?"

"Nobody knows," I said dramatically, mysteriously. "Come here, I want to show you something."

I grabbed his hand, which felt as big as a ham, and led him down the hall and through the kitchen and into the empty garage, over to the orange XXX door. We paused before it. I was breathing hard.

"Do you know what this is?" I asked him.

"You sure are pretty," Harlan said loudly. This announcement appeared to surprise him as much as it surprised me. He immediately turned fiery red and ducked his head and started stamping his feet in their big uncool work boots.

Hick, I thought. *Swamp boy.* "Come on," I said, and pulled the door up and pushed him ahead of me, down the stairs. "This is the Bomb Shelter," I said.

"No kidding," Harlan said. "Well, I'll be darned."

I was thrilled to see the entwined rattlesnakes on the back of his jacket disappearing into the gloom. I shut the door behind myself and followed, showing him everything: the Geiger counter, the supplies, etc., though I did not go into any details about the chemical toilet.

"Let's sit here." I patted the pile of mattresses. "Let me get you something to drink." I opened a can of orange juice for him and one for myself and clinked mine against his in a toast. "Cheers!" I said. I knew my sophistication was knocking him out. He just kept grinning at me, forgetting to drink his juice, while I downed mine in one sophisticated gulp and broke open a package of Fig Newtons.

"Care for a cookie?" I said, knowing that cousin Glenda would kill me. "A little refreshment?" There in the humming blue light of the Bomb Shelter, I turned into the perfect hostess, exactly as prescribed in *Teen* magazine. ("When he comes to your home, have refreshments ready.")

Harlan Boyd set his juice can down carefully on the Sterno stove. "C'mere," he said.

I didn't think about being good or not being good. I didn't think about anything. I dropped the Fig Newtons on the floor and scooted over there to get myself kissed by a boy for the first time ever, and I have to say it was just fine, and the whole world dropped out from under me for I don't know how long while Harlan Boyd and I mashed our lips together, mouths closed, and then open as he stuck his tongue into mine. (*Teen* magazine had not mentioned tongues.) I was lying partway back on the mattress by now, with him on top of me, when suddenly I felt this hard thing like a stick between us. What was it? I struggled upward like a swimmer surfacing through thousands of feet of water. *Uh-oh.* What would Jesus think of *that*?

But it was all over, anyway, because cousin Glenda's station wagon pulled into the garage, and then we could hear the car doors slamming and cousin Glenda and Rayette calling my name, getting closer and closer. Of course, cousin Glenda knew where I was. Cousin Glenda knew everything.

Since there was no other way to get out of the Bomb Shelter, Harlan and I just sat there side by side, buddies at the end of the world, until the orange door opened and cousin Glenda came clomping downstairs like the wrath of God.

BY THE TIME Daddy appeared to retrieve me, Christmas had come and gone and I had repented of my behavior in the Bomb Shelter and was being totally good again, or as good as possible, newly aware of my potential for backsliding. Harlan Boyd never spoke to me again. He dropped out of Tri-Hi-Y and wouldn't even look at me in math class, where he got a D-minus for the semester.

It was over. I knew he still loved me, though, with a hopeless love, the kind of love my uncle Mason had felt for his wife, a love so strong it had caused him to go out and cut somebody. I didn't think Harlan would do that, though I sort of wished he would. But he was too nice. Also, he had basketball practice every day after school, so he was very busy. Anyway, I would be far, far away soon, in Key West, Florida, where Mama and Daddy were going to "patch up their marriage": a geographical cure prescribed by Mama's doctors.

But I hated to leave Repass. This astonished Mama and Daddy, who looked puzzled as they stood waiting while I sobbed, hugging first Rayette and then cousin Glenda. Raymond stood like a tree by the door. "Now come on, Jennifer."

Cousin Glenda finally disentangled herself from my frantic arms. "What did I tell you?"

I had to smile.

Rayette smiled.

"*Get a grip*," we all said together, and I started laughing in spite of my tears.

E VEN THOUGH DADDY had bought us a new car for the occasion, a silvery-gray fishtailed Cadillac, the long drive down to Florida was grim. Mama and Daddy sat up front, and I had the wide backseat all to myself. There was a seat divider, which I could pull down to make a table if I wanted to draw or write. I had a shopping bag containing a white New Testament with my name embossed on the front in gold, a good-bye gift from my cousins; a copy of '*Twixt Twelve and Twenty* by Pat Boone, a gift from my grandmother; Rayette's Rattler yearbook from the year before; the yellow blouse I had made in 4-H; and *The Search for Bridey Murphy*, which I had been dying to get my hands on. Mama had just finished reading it. At the bottom of the shopping bag was my old jewelry box, all locked up, and a big new auxiliary jewelry box containing the stale package of Fig Newtons and the empty orange juice can touched by Harlan Boyd. I had resurrected my notebook and brought it along, too, to record my thoughts and observations, though I had still given up both espionage and literature at least for the time being, until I could get my parents through this crisis.

I had made a new chart in the back of my notebook. It said "Good Deeds" at the top and then had the days of February numbered down the left-hand margin with a line drawn out from each date. I had done this laboriously, with a ruler, before leaving my cousins'. We would be gone for one whole month, and I planned to do a good deed every day—twenty-eight good deeds, which ought to be enough to bring even Mama and Daddy back together.

I had my work cut out for me. It would be a challenge. Mama and Daddy sat as far apart as possible from each other on the big front seat, as remote as planets. They were both smoking a lot (Mama, Newports; Daddy, Winstons), making the air in the new Cadillac dense and blue and wavy, making my eyes water all the way down through South Carolina and Georgia, until it grew warm enough in Florida for us to crack the windows.

Cousin Glenda's reaction upon seeing Mama had been the same as mine: "Oh, Billie, you poor thing!" for Mama had simply lost her luster. She had become a thinner, paler version of herself, quieter and more hesitant. Cousin Glenda's final instructions for us ("Now you all just forget about everything and have a good time, you hear me?") seemed more and more impossible to follow, the farther we traveled.

It became clear that I was absolutely necessary to this trip, as the only remaining link between Mama and Daddy. They were trying to patch up their marriage for me, and the only way to do it seemed to be *through me*. So I was consulted on everything: where to spend the night, for instance, hotel or motel? I picked the Palm Courts, a pink stucco motel where Mama and I shared a tiny square room and bath, while Daddy had the same to himself. Mama got ready for bed as if she were in a trance—brushing her teeth, creaming her face with Noxzema, taking a lot of pills. As my good deed, I folded up the clothes she had just thrown over a chair, and was rewarded for this when she put them all back on the next morning, the same exact outfit— something she would never have done in the past.

My parents asked me where we should eat lunch, whether to play the radio or not, whether to stop at the Bok Singing Tower or not (no), whether to stop at Weeki Wachee Springs or not (yes). I loved Weeki Wachee Springs, where beautiful girls swam around in underwater caverns with oxygen tanks on their backs, among the brilliant angelfish. I determined to go back when I was grown and get a swimming job.

My parents did not come with me into the underwater viewing room at Weeki Wachee Springs. They did not appear to be at all interested in the girl divers, or the fish, or anything. They sat on the low stone wall outside the entrance waiting patiently for me to emerge, not talking, smoking. They looked like prisoners blinking in the sun. I made them wait an extra hour, until shark-feeding time, and they didn't even complain about that.

This is when I realized that I could make them do anything I wanted on this trip. *Anything.* I was in charge.

Mama pulled out her compact and looked at herself the minute we got back in the car after Weeki Wachee Springs. "Oh, no!" she started sobbing. "I got *sunburned!* I didn't think I could get sunburned so early in the year, but this Florida sun is just so *hot* . . ." Mama went on and on. I didn't see what she was all upset about, myself, but at least it was more than she had said so far on the whole trip. "Honey, ask your daddy if he can get me some Solarcaine and some more Noxzema," she said to me.

"Daddy, can you do that?" I said to Daddy, who pulled off at the very next drugstore, a huge Rexall with a big Coppertone sign over it.

"I'll go in," I volunteered, and Mama thrust a ten dollar bill over the seat at me.

"No, I'll go, Jenny," Daddy said.

"No, *I'll do it*, Daddy!" I had already decided to count this as my good deed for the day. "Solarcaine and Noxzema, right?" Daddy jumped out of the car and made a grab for the money, but I danced away, waving it. "I'll be back in a minute," I yelled.

"Damn it," Daddy said.

"Jenny, get me some more cigarettes, too," Mama called after me.

I took off.

"God damn it," Daddy said behind me.

I got the Solarcaine and the Noxzema (a smell I will forever associate with Mama), plus some peanut M&M's for myself, and went back to the car, where Mama sat bowed with her head in her hands and Daddy stood leaning against his door, smoking furiously. They had been arguing, I could tell. The words hung in the Florida air. They had started arguing probably the very minute I disappeared into the Rexall. I couldn't leave them alone for even a minute! What a responsibility! I went around to Mama's side of the car and put the paper bag from the Rexall and the wad of change in her lap. "Oh, honey, just keep the change," she said, so I put it in my pocket along with the M&M's. Good deeds are always rewarded, as cousin Glenda had told me.

"Did you forget my cigarettes?" Mama asked.

I cleared my throat. "No," I said, fidgeting from one foot to the other. "You don't need any more cigarettes, either one of you," I announced. "You are both smoking too much, and you'll make yourselves sick."

Mama gasped and started to cry.

Daddy walked around the fancy front grillework of the Cadillac. "Now listen here, Miss," he said, "you don't talk to your mother that way, in case you've forgotten. You apologize to her, and get in the damn car, and let's get the hell out of here." He looked at his watch as if we had some big schedule to keep, but I knew we didn't have any schedule at all.

I stood my ground. "Don't say 'hell,'" I said. "You curse too much, too."

"Now just a minute," Daddy said. "What's going on here?" For the first time, he really looked at me.

Mama stuck her head out the window and squinted at me, too—suddenly seeming, in spite of her puffy eyes, almost herself again. "Just what *is* going on here?" she asked. "And take off that damn cross, for God's sake, Jenny. Where in the world did you get that ugly old thing, anyway?"

"Don't say 'for God's sake,'" I said. "What would Jesus think of that?"

"*Get in the goddamn car!*" Daddy was gritting his teeth.

I got in and slammed the door and prayed that Jesus would not punish Mama and Daddy for taking His name in vain, and that I could stay good enough for long enough to get them back together, and that Rayette would not miss her cross too much.

CENTRAL FLORIDA WAS pretty boring, but I loved Miami, with lots of traffic and lots of people in the streets shouting and gesturing, speaking Spanish. "Lock all the doors," Mama instructed. "Jenny, don't stare." I couldn't help it as we cruised slowly through the city in our huge, shiny, smoke-filled car like a shark at Weeki Wachee Springs, like a submarine from another civilization.

My father never took his eyes off the road ahead. He seemed infinitely, infinitely sad to me, full of his grim resolve. He was doing the only thing he *could* do—I see this now—given the time and the place they lived in, and the circumstances, and all the women who depended upon him, and all the people at the mill, which Mr. Kinney was gamely running even now, in Daddy's absence. For my father, being the man he was, no other choice was possible.

And Mama—what was *she* thinking over there with her pretty blond cap of curls and her milk-glass baby-doll face wreathed in smoke, so far from everything familiar? Did she really want to patch up her marriage? Did she even understand that she had any choice in the matter? I couldn't tell. She remained vacant-eyed and silent. When they spoke to each other, it was with an exaggerated politeness that I soon adopted, too, as if we were *all* sick.

The drive was interminable. Finally I asked Daddy why we were going *there* for our prescribed vacation, anyway, when there were so many other places to go that were so much closer. "Well, Jenny," Daddy said, "you know I was in the Navy"— I nodded— "in fact, I met your mother when I was in the Navy, stationed in Charleston"—I nodded again, while Mama merely widened her big blue eyes as if this were news to her— "and before Charleston, I was stationed in Key West, and I'll tell you, I've always wanted to go back. It's not like anywhere else, you'll see. It's very exotic. I thought it would be good for us to take a trip together to someplace completely different, the three of us, after what we've been through this past year. I thought we could use a little adventure."

Daddy stubbed out his cigarette as he said "adventure," glancing over at Mama. She looked out the window. I was mad at him for saying "what we've been through this past year," as if none of it were his own fault, as if we'd all been hit by a truck. I had to rub my cross and count backward from one hundred in order to stay good, to keep from saying something mean.

It was easier once we could see the water. This happened after Miami. Suddenly we were on a bridge with blue water under us and on either side, and then we were on Route 1. "Originally the only way you could get to Key West was by boat or by rail, Jenny. A man named Henry Flagler started the railroad in 1905, and it took him seven years to get all the way down to Key West. You can still see the tracks right over there, see that old trestle? A storm blew the railroad away sometime in the thirties," Daddy was saying, when Mama started to shriek.

"Key Largo! Look, John, that sign says Key Largo! You didn't tell me we were going to Key Largo, John. Oh, Jenny, isn't this exciting?"

I sat up. *Key Largo* was one of Mama's and my all-time favorite movies.

"Oh, *stop*, John! I want to take a picture."

Mama had a brand-new Brownie camera, which Daddy had bought her especially for this trip, but until now she hadn't shown any interest in it. We had to pull over on the sandy side of the road while she rummaged through her overnight case to find it, and then Daddy had to read the instructions to figure out how to load it. I shaded my eyes from the sun and breathed in the fishy air and looked at a long-legged bird that hopped nearer and nearer. It expected us to give it something, so I got a nab out of Mama's pocketbook. Mama freshened her lipstick and fluffed up her curls.

"Okay, now." She walked over and leaned against the sign that said 'Key Largo' and smiled, a big red smile that came out of nowhere.

Daddy snapped the picture.

"Now you get in it *with me*, honey," she said to me, and I

did, and Daddy took that picture, too. I still have it. There's a palm tree behind us, and the sun is in our eyes. Then we all got back in the car and drove through Key Largo, which wasn't much, as it turned out. It only took about two minutes.

"I'm not sure they actually filmed it here," said Daddy, who knew they hadn't.

"Oh, of course they did!" Mama said. "It's named *Key Largo*, isn't it? *Silly.*" For a moment, she sounded like herself again.

Humphrey Bogart had died of cancer not even two years earlier, in 1957, ending a marriage that Mama and I were just crazy about. We knew the facts by heart. Everybody had thought Lauren Bacall was too young for him when they met in 1943 (she was only nineteen, he was forty-four), but they had been blissfully happy together, against all odds, and she had nursed him devotedly when he got cancer; on his death-bed, Bogey's last words were for her: "Good-bye, kid." Lauren Bacall never got over him, of course. How could she? I thought about it. Clark Gable never got over Carole Lombard, either, after she died in that tragic plane crash, though he *tried* to. He kept marrying other people, but nobody else ever really *took*. And what about Spencer Tracy, who loved Katharine Hepburn for years yet never left his wife?

Then I had this awful thought: Why should it be any different for Daddy and Carroll Byrd? What if Daddy was just *pretending* to patch up the marriage, knowing he would never be able to live without Carroll Byrd? Or what if he was really *trying* to give her up, and couldn't? What if he just *couldn't*? I watched him carefully as he drove us down the Keys. But unlike Mama, who was all on the surface, all open, too open, I could never guess what Daddy was thinking. His face betrayed nothing.

We ate lunch at a place called the Green Turtle Inn, which had a cannery (named Sid and Roxie's) right across the road, where they canned turtle meat. Yuck! It was on the menu, too—turtle steak, turtle soup. Daddy ordered the turtle soup. Mama ordered a Manhattan and a cup of clam chowder, staring defiantly at Daddy. I ordered a hamburger. It was a confusing, jumbled-up restaurant, with tables and chairs that didn't match, and all kinds of people, some of them very loud. Nobody was dressed up. It was not like any restaurant I had been to before. As we were leaving, a fight broke out at the bar. "Don't look at anybody," Mama said, clutching my shoulder and pushing me ahead of her, and we got out of there, and we did not look at anybody, or mention Mason.

None of us mentioned Mason's death, or Mama's stay in the hospital, or Carroll Byrd. All the way down the Keys, what we did not say seemed as real as what we did say, like the shadowy railroad alongside the highway with its ghost bridges spanning the sea. I kept wishing cousin Glenda had come along, to haul everything out in the open and pray over it.

STARTED GETTING REALLY excited on the Seven Mile Bridge, a span so long over a stretch of water so wide that it seemed we were entering another world. It had not occurred to me that water could be so many different colors of blue. I saw dark shadows (sharks? rays?) moving under it, and cloud shadows moving over it.

We touched land briefly at Bahia Honda, then crossed the water again to Big Pine. Daddy solemnly read the road signs out loud to us, as if he were a travel guide or we were illiterate: Little Torch Key, Niles Channel, Summerland Key, Cudjoe, Sugarloaf. By now I had abandoned even *Bridey Murphy* and was sitting up against the front seat, so I could see everything as soon as they did.

We crossed Stock Island and drove into Key West around suppertime. After the long stretches of water and the scruffy unpopulated keys we'd come through, Key West was disorienting, a bright buzz of color and noise.

"Did *you* have a uniform like that?" I asked Daddy as a young sailor dodged in front of our big car.

"Pretty much," Daddy said. "In fact, that young man might

have been me, thirty years ago." This thought seemed to make him sad. He cleared his throat and went on. "You'll see a lot of Navy personnel here right now because of the situation in Cuba, which is only ninety miles away. A dictator named Batista has just been ousted, and the rebels have taken over."

"Castro, right?" I already knew about this from the *Weekly Readers* we had to read in civics class at Repass Junior High.

Daddy looked impressed. "Why, that's right, Jenny. Fidel Castro is the rebel leader, a genuine hero." Daddy was always for the people, for the underdog. His own father had kept the union out of the mill, but after Granddaddy killed himself, Daddy welcomed it. This was only one of Grandmother's many longtime grievances against Daddy.

We stopped for the red light at Truman and White, which gave me a chance to get a good look at all the boys in uniform along the sidewalk. Several of them were as cute as Harlan Boyd, in that same sweet country way, which made me feel funny deep down in my stomach. But nobody was as cute as Tom Burlington. Nobody would ever be as cute as Tom Burlington.

"Well, I like Ike," Mama said irrelevantly. This had something to do with Castro, I believe.

It was the kind of remark that used to make Daddy smile, or pinch her cheek. Not now. Instead, he curled his lip in an ugly way. Luckily Mama did not notice; she was staring out the open window. "I just wish you'd look at all these flowers!" she said. "I have never seen such vines."

I hadn't, either. Nor had I ever seen anyplace that looked

like Key West, with old frame houses covered and sometimes hidden by lush vegetation, with dogs and cats and chickens running around in the streets, and piano music and laughter pouring out of open doorways. I had never seen adults riding bicycles before, yet it seemed to be a common form of transportation here. People sat on their porches and balconies or stood chatting on the sidewalks beneath big-leafed trees. The light was green and golden. Everybody seemed to have all the time in the world.

I observed these people carefully.

Nobody looked like us.

"We're almost there," Daddy said.

Mama reapplied her lipstick. We turned left onto Duval Street, and now I could see a glistening patch of ocean ahead. Daddy pulled into a motel called the Blue Marlin, with a huge fish on its sign. Mama and I waited in the car, under the entrance portico, while he headed for the office, tucking his shirt down in back as he went. The motel was made of blue-painted concrete, two stories in a U shape around a good-size pool featuring a diving board and a water slide and lots of lounge chairs and palm trees. "Wow, this is really nice, isn't it?" I said to Mama, who was lighting a cigarette and didn't answer. Still, I was hopeful. The Blue Marlin *was* nice. But was it nice enough to get Mama and Daddy back together? Mama smoked that whole cigarette and lit another, blowing smoke rings out her window. I watched a neon-green lizard zip up a blue concrete wall.

"Why is this *taking so long?*" Mama said finally. She looked like she was about to cry.

I was halfway out of the car, on my way to find out, when Daddy came through the plate-glass doors jingling two keys, with a funny look on his face. "Jenny, get back in the car," he said abruptly, and I did. Then Daddy got in and closed his door and turned to look at us instead of starting the car.

"You're not going to believe this, Billie," he said slowly.

"What? What is it? Are the girls okay?" Mama's pretty face was an instant mask of alarm. She had had too much bad news.

"Oh no, nothing like that." Daddy smiled his new, distant smile. "It appears that almost this entire motel has been taken over by the cast and crew of a movie that they are shooting on location right now in Key West, over at the Navy yard. There are only four rooms they're not occupying, and it turns out we've got two of them." Daddy jingled his keys again. "They asked me a lot of questions. I had to swear that we weren't journalists or photographers in order to stay here."

"Who did you say we are?" I asked. It was exactly what I had been trying to figure out.

Daddy looked at me. "An American family," he said firmly. I felt something very deep inside myself relax. "But Jenny," he added in a no-nonsense voice, "I promised that man that you *would not bother* the stars, do you hear me? Or the crew, or anybody else. I promised because I knew that you and your mother would want to stay here. There are no other children at this motel, so you'll just have to amuse yourself. You can meet some other kids down there, I imagine"—Daddy pointed to the beach at the end of the street—"but you can't bring them here, and you *cannot* bother anybody at this motel. Is that clear?" He had his key in the ignition, yet did not turn it. I knew he was speaking as much to Mama as to me.

"Yes," I said.

"Which stars?" Mama asked.

"Well, there's Dina Merrill," Daddy said, "and Tony Curtis . . ."

"Tony Curtis!" Mama and I squealed together. Tony Curtis had just been voted the most popular young actor in Hollywood, after the recent success of *The Defiant Ones.* Mama and I were crazy about Tony Curtis.

Daddy had to grin in spite of himself. "And you just missed Janet Leigh," he said. "She left yesterday. She was here for two weeks, apparently, on vacation. She's not in this movie, though."

"She's gone back to California to be with the children," Mama said automatically. "Kelly and Jamie."

Daddy looked at her for a while. Then he cleared his throat and said, "That's not all."

"Who?" Mama and I breathed together. Over the top of the seat, I clutched her hand.

"Cary Grant." Daddy was trying to sound offhand.

"Cary Grant!" We couldn't believe it. The most gorgeous, the most elegant, the biggest star in Hollywood!

"He's got the bungalow and several of those end units." Daddy pointed. "His secretary is here, and a number of other people, his whole staff. The man at the desk says he's a real gentleman."

"Of course he is," Mama said.

I was not so sure of that. I sucked in my breath, thinking of his recent affair with Sophia Loren.

Mama and I peered in Cary Grant's direction but couldn't see any particular activity over there beyond the pool and the pink bougainvillea, which grew in profusion, shielding the bungalow.

"They're still on location today," Daddy said. "They don't get back until about eight o'clock. They're filming down at the Navy yard, where they've painted a submarine pink for this movie. The movie is called *Operation Petticoat*. So if everything is understood, Jenny"—I bobbed my head vigorously—"then let's get unpacked, girls!" Daddy finally started the car and drove around back.

Our rooms were on the second floor. I insisted on helping Daddy carry the bags, even though he said I didn't have to. It was my good deed for the day. My room, 208, had a connecting door into Mama and Daddy's room, 209, which was actually a suite with two beds and a rattan settee and coffee table and two armchairs and a tiny kitchenette. I was utterly charmed by the kitchenette, with its two-burner stovetop and miniature refrigerator. It had four of everything—four spoons, four forks, four knives, four plates, four glasses.

"You can go swimming before supper if you want to," Mama told me, so I went in my room and put on my bathing suit and headed for the pool, while Daddy fixed gin and tonics for himself and Mama and pulled two chairs out onto the balcony.

"Honestly, John," Mama was saying behind me as I took off down the concrete stairs, "is that really true, about the movie company? Or did you make all that up?"

"Scout's honor, Billie," Daddy said.

At least they were talking to each other.

I took a running dive into the water.

I F WE RARELY saw Cary Grant, it was not from lack of trying. He had his own chef, and took his meals mostly in his bungalow, where he held private parties as well. He rode to and from the set in a chauffeured limousine, which had been written into his contract, according to Mr. Rudy, the motel manager, our informer. Sometimes I sneaked out to the parking lot in the early morning to wash the windshield and polish the hubcaps of the limousine, though I was discouraged in this particular good deed by Rocco Bacco, Mr. Grant's chauffeur.

Cary Grant often gave other cast members, and the pretty young script girls and makeup girls, a ride in the limousine. Mama considered this very democratic of him; she pronounced him a "perfect gentleman." I was a little disappointed in his looks, personally. He was so old, for one thing. I thought he looked pretty much like any other old guy, for instance Dr. Nevins, our family physician back in Lewisville, or Ronnie Tuttle, Aunt Judy's first husband. Cary Grant was not even as good-looking as Daddy.

I *did* like his accent, however. I liked the way he said "hot dog" on the night they had the cast cookout by the pool. He said "hot dog" as if the *o*'s were long instead of short. Mama said this was English. On the night of the cookout, Mama and I sat on our balcony, suspended over the crowd, so we could see everything: the gorgeous girls in their two-piece bathing suits, the muscly young men, two guys with beards (was one of them the director?), the tall bitchy woman with red hair and glasses who seemed to be in charge of herding everybody around. We were there to see her break into a terrible tap dance (everybody clapped politely) and to see Tony Curtis do his Cary Grant imitation at Mr. Grant's request, and then to see Tony Curtis get thrown in the pool by most of the crew, who soon joined him, swimming around in their clothes. Mama and I pulled our chairs up to the rail and hung over it to watch. By then it was dark and the lighted aqua pool glowed like a jewel in the fragrant night, full of impossibly attractive people trailing wet clothes through the water.

Mama nudged me. "Hollywood high jinks," she said.

Behind us, in their room, Daddy lay on one of the beds reading some big book, a biography. Sometimes he seemed amused by our reaction to the movie stars; other times he seemed disgusted; and that night, when we wouldn't leave our vantage point to go out for dinner, he had gone without us. We didn't care. We were perfectly happy to have potato chips and Fritos for dinner. We weren't about to leave the balcony, that was for sure, especially after they all jumped into the pool. I thought they might peel off their clothes at any moment, but nobody did. The party broke up soon after the swimming part. People disappeared into their rooms or sat quietly in the lounge chairs around the pool, where there were so many plants and it was so dark that Mama and I couldn't see who they were anymore; all we could see was the occasional flare of a match, and all we could hear was a low laugh now and then.

In fact, we never did see as many high jinks as we expected. The biggest surprise about the movie business was how hard everybody worked. The bus was waiting under the portico every morning at seven-thirty; by seven forty-five, everybody, even Cary Grant, was gone.

Though I was always there to witness their departure, it was much too early for Mama, who had to make do with peeping from behind the venetian blinds. Then she'd fall back asleep for two more hours while Daddy took a long walk around the island or went fishing with Captain Tony. This left me free to roam the streets, or swim in the pool, or talk to Mr. Rudy, or do anything else I wanted, and often I'd fit in my good deed right then, so I'd have it over with.

Sometimes I walked around the corner to the big scary church and prayed with the Catholics. I loved the gory statues and the candles. I loved the feel of the scratchy cold stone floor on my knees when I knelt to pray. I loved the old people dressed in black, bent over and mumbling their prayers. Where did all these old people come from, anyway? I never saw them on the beach or in the streets, that's for sure. They looked dark and sad. I knew they would die soon. The Jesus in the Catholic statues was a lot less peppy than the one back at St. Michael's—and certainly than the Jesus in my cousins' church in Repass, who looked like a Ken doll. *This* Jesus' brow was encircled by thorns, and He was always bleeding.

It was hard to imagine what He would think of anything. He was too busy suffering.

But I loved the way *I* felt, clean and new and bursting with goodness, when I popped back out of that church into the sunny Key West morning, like a girl in a cuckoo clock. I always took some money to donate, and if I could scrounge up enough, I'd buy a candle from the sad lady and light it in honor of my uncle Mason and Carroll Byrd and Harlan Boyd. Whenever I did this, I'd check in throughout the day to see my candle flickering in its red glass holder in the bank of candles burning in the alcove. I liked to see how long my candle would last in comparison with the others, and make sure I got my money's worth. The money came from Daddy, who left change from his pockets scattered on top of the bureau. I'd gather this up and take it with me on my morning good-deed run.

Other times I'd give the money away to the bums who slept on the beach at the end of the street, or to the children who lived on top of the Cuban grocery where I went to buy cigarettes for Mama and café con leche for myself. I came to love café con leche, and usually that was what I'd have for breakfast, café con leche and a Hershey bar.

It thrilled me to walk down the alley behind the Havana Madrid nightclub, where strippers worked and "unimaginable things" went on in the back room, according to Mama.

One of the signs on the front of the club said LIVE BOTTOM-
LESS, FRIDAY ONLY—a show I'd have given anything to see.
By mid-morning, the strippers were often out on a wooden
porch behind the nightclub, sunning themselves and smoking
cigarettes and giggling like high school girls. Two of them,
sisters maybe, even looked like high school girls, not much
older than I.

One day they were sitting together on a ratty chaise longue,
looking at a fashion magazine, when I came walking along.
"Hi!" I said loudly, on impulse. Immediately I could feel myself turning red all over.

"Hi!" they said right back. They jumped up and came to
the rail. Their fresh morning faces, without makeup, were
open and friendly. "Me Luisa," the thin one said. "Me Rosa,"
said the other, blinking into the sun. Over the rail, they stared
at me curiously. I felt like an exhibit—an American Girl,
member of an American Family, suddenly exotic in this locale.

"Me Jenny," I said, thumping my chest in a gesture so awk-
ward it made us all break into giggles.

"You smoke a cigarette?" Luisa offered her crumpled pack
of Camels.

I loved the way she said "seegarette," and resolved on the
spot to say it that way for the rest of my life.

"Don't mind if I do," I said, and took one.

"Rosa! Luisa! What are you doing? This little girl doesn't
smoke!" An older woman wearing a purple silk kimono stepped
up behind them. She had a hard leathery face and dyed red hair.

"Oh yes I do," I assured her, putting the cigarette in the pocket of my camp shirt. "I've just been trying to quit."

The woman grinned at me. "You have, huh?" she said. "Well, as long as you're here, why don't you make yourself useful, and get me a newspaper." She flipped me a fifty-cent piece.

When I came back with the paper, she said, "Aw, honey, keep the change," and I did. Then I got to go up on the porch and sit in a chair and smoke my cigarette and get my stubby fingernails painted by Rosa, who was doing everybody's, while the woman turned to the crossword puzzle and worked it in a flash, just like Daddy. Her name was Red.

Rosa and Luisa had other, stripper names (Candy Love, Nookie) for their acts. The billboard on the sidewalk in front of the Havana Madrid featured a photograph of Luisa/Nookie, wearing only a G-string. She was much too thin, with no breasts to speak of. (Rayette could have made a fortune at the Havana Madrid.) Luisa and Rosa both looked tired, too. I was always worried about their health.

Sometimes I brought them oranges, and one morning I left a bottle of vitamins for them on the porch rail. The bottle had disappeared by afternoon, but Rosa and Luisa never mentioned the vitamins to me. Of course, they didn't know I was the person who had brought them. But this didn't matter; it was still a good deed.

Another place I loved to go was the graveyard, where I could always clean off a grave or two. There were about a million graves over there, a million people buried above the ground in white concrete boxes that you could walk on or sit on, and some of them had not been cleaned off for the longest time, you could tell. You could tell that nobody cared about those people anymore at all. Maybe everyone who ever knew them was dead. I'd push the brown leaves into little piles, then scrape green mold off them with the snow scraper from Daddy's new car. Then I'd walk around the graveyard admiring the statues—swans, angels, lambs, cutoff tree trunks, and even some stone dogs on dogs' graves. *Those dogs are all dead now*, I'd think, and a thrill would shoot through me. I liked to subtract the dates and figure out how long the people had lived and try to imagine what they had died of. I liked to read the names and inscriptions, my favorite being:

HERE LIES OUR HEART

What if I died right now? What if I was hit by a car on my way back to the motel? What would they write on *my* grave? I hoped it would be "Our Jenny, a good girl." The very thought of this made me cry and cry. Mason's stone had only his full name on it, Henry Mason Rutledge, and the dates of his birth and death, and the carving of a bird in flight. They had buried him in our family plot at St. Michael's next to Granddaddy who had killed himself, and a whole bunch of other old dead people in our family, people so old that even their names were all but gone from their stones. I wanted to be buried in the nifty aboveground graveyard in Key West, and informed

Mama of this one morning when I got back to the motel and found her out sunning by the pool.

She took off her dark glasses and sat up in the lounge chair to stare at me. "You what, honey?" she said.

"Bury me in Key West," I said. "In case I die, I mean. I want to be buried in the cemetery here, in one of those cool white concrete boxes, with an angel. A big angel."

"Oh, honestly, Jenny, where do you get these crazy ideas? And for heaven's sake, take off that awful blouse," Mama said. "I swear, it looks like somebody *made* it."

WE FELL INTO a routine. I'd go fishing with Daddy, and I'd shop or sun or watch the movie stars with Mama. This way, I got to have plenty of everybody's undivided attention, though I kept wishing my parents would do more things together. Sometimes they did, though Daddy always looked like a man fulfilling a duty, even after Mama started wearing flowers in her hair.

I loved those rare nights they went out without me. I'd swim in the pool or run errands for Mr. Rudy or smoke Mama's cigarettes or hide in the shrubbery by the pool in order to keep up with several romances I had taken an interest in. Then, of course, I would have to do a lot of good deeds to make up for all that. Then I'd read *East of Eden*, which somebody had carelessly left by the pool (I had finished *Bridey Murphy*), and then I'd have to read my New Testament to make up for *that*. I was really busy, and was often completely exhausted by my efforts.

I couldn't tell whether or not the good deeds were working. My parents were endlessly cordial to each other now, but so far they had never slept in the same bed. I knew this for a fact. I checked their room every morning.

So I doubled my efforts—buying more candles, cleaning more graves, using up all Mama's Kleenex on Cary Grant's hubcaps, donating a jar of her Noxzema to the Havana Madrid girls. But we seemed to have reached a stalemate. Entranced by the stars, Mama was becoming herself again. But would this ever be enough for Daddy? Could it be? I knew that Frank Sinatra still loved Ava Gardner right now, even though she was now in Spain living with a bullfighter. The bullfighter meant nothing to Frank. He was peanuts; he was toast. Frank would *always* love Ava.

I prayed it would not be so for Daddy and Carroll Byrd.

It was hard to stay mad at Daddy, however. His lawyer-like quality of paying close attention was flattering; he was winning me over again. I especially liked our fishing trips. Once we got up at four a.m. to drive up the Keys and go out with a one-eyed man named Captain Lewjack who gave me a mug of black coffee and a jelly glass of brandy and strapped me into a fighting chair and kept chanting, "C'mon, baby, c'mon, baby, hootchie-koo," when I hooked a dolphin.

"Not a *dolphin!*" I cried out at first, though Daddy and Captain Lewjack assured me it wasn't *that* kind of dolphin but the other kind, a game fish. Still, the dolphin was so beautiful that it took my breath away when it leaped out of the water for the first time, its lovely colors like a rainbow in the sun. It turned iron gray the instant Captain Lewjack hit it on the head with a hammer after I pulled it in, with Daddy's help.

This was the same day Daddy caught a marlin after a three-hour struggle, and I still have the photograph that was taken of him and the marlin on the dock when we went back in: Daddy bare-chested and grinning from ear to ear, cigarette dangling from the corner of his mouth, wearing a Panama hat. It is impossible to tell that he had a broken heart, or that anything at all was the matter with him.

I have another photograph, of myself beside a giant jewfish which I hooked when we went out on Captain Tony's party boat. This picture ran in the Key West newspaper, even though I didn't actually catch the fish: it was brought up with block and tackle by several of Captain Tony's crew members. It was the ugliest fish I had ever seen. In the picture, I'm nearly invisible behind somebody's enormous sunglasses; the caption reads "Va. Miss Gets Big Jew."

Daddy and I were fools for fish. We also took the glass bottom boat trip out to the reef, where we peered down into another world, another universe, with its softly waving sea fans and giant brain coral and gorgeous deadly fire coral and silly octopuses and squids with big round doll baby eyes. Daddy took me to the old aquarium at Mallory square, and later I went again and again by myself. I liked to touch the barracudas and turtles. I especially liked the sharks, and never tired of leaning way over their open pen to watch them glide by (constantly, endlessly, they *could not* be still), knowing that they would kill me if they could. They would *love* to kill me, and I loved to think about this. For a nickel, you could feed them, which counted as one good deed.

What I did with Mama never varied. Shortly before nine o'clock every evening, just after dinner, we'd go into the lobby of the Blue Marlin and settle ourselves on a large rattan sofa, which she called "the davenport."

"'Lo, Miz Billie," Hal, the skinny night clerk, would say, and Mama always said, "How are you, Hal?" as if she really cared. Now restored to something approaching her old self again, Mama had everybody at the motel eating out of her hand. Hal adored her. Everyone did.

Mama carried a newspaper. I carried a magazine or a book. (Once I brought my New Testament, but Mama said, "Honestly, Jenny! Take that thing back to your room," rolling her eyes, so I did.) We'd sit down ostentatiously on the davenport and begin to read. Right behind us stood a row of potted plants. Right behind them stood a table with an ashtray and a telephone on it, the only telephone at the Blue Marlin available for guests to use. An old armchair was next to the table.

And every night, at exactly nine o'clock, here came Tony Curtis through the plate-glass doors. He nodded to Hal, then walked to the table, where he sat down and lifted the receiver and asked for a long-distance operator. Mama rattled her paper, reading. Sometimes there'd be a brief wait, during which Tony lit a cigarette, until Janet Leigh answered the phone in Hollywood, all the way across the continent.

"Hello, darling," Tony said.

Mama sighed. I sighed. We kept on reading.

Tony talked about what had happened on the set that day;

he referred to Cary Grant as a fine fellow. Then he'd ask about the kids, and about the rest of the family, and about their friends. They seemed to have a lot of friends. Sometimes they'd talk about really boring things, such as money. Janet Leigh always had a lot to say, and Tony chuckled intimately into the phone and smoked another cigarette while he listened to her. Then he always told her how much he missed her. At this point Mama and I would take deep breaths and straighten up: here came the moment we were waiting for.

First Tony said, "I love you," and then listened, while (we guessed) Janet Leigh said, "I love you," back.

Then he said, "God bless you, darling," and hung up.

By then Mama was breathing so hard she could barely hold her paper, and I felt just as I had felt in the Bomb Shelter when Harlan Boyd stuck his tongue in my mouth. Mama and I were so rattled that we didn't even notice when Tony Curtis strode back through the lobby and out the door. "Thanks, Hal," he'd say, giving Hal a mock salute. Tony Curtis was *so cute*. I even thought old buck-toothed Hal was cute, by then. I thought everybody was cute.

Romance was in the very air here—in the lush bright flowers, the seductive vines, the lazy twirling overhead fans, the snatches of song on the soft, soft breeze. Surely Mama and Daddy would *catch it* somehow. Surely they would fall in love again.

I had everything riding on this.

Then came the big night—when Tony Curtis had just said, "God bless you, darling," and Mama and I were still in a fever state—the night that Tony Curtis paused before going out the door and then turned on his heel in a military way (his role was that of Navy Lieutenant Nick Holden) and walked to the davenport, right up to Mama and me. He was wearing white shorts and a red knit shirt, I will never forget. He cleared his throat. "Ladies?" he said.

Mama and I went on reading as though our lives depended on it.

"Ladies?" Tony Curtis said again.

I looked up into those famous blue eyes and suddenly had to pee.

Mama folded her newspaper and stuck out her hand.

"I'm Billie Dale, from Virginia," she said, "and this is my daughter Jenny."

Tony Curtis shook Mama's hand, bowing slightly from the waist, and then took mine. "So pleased to meet you," he said. He was smiling. "From Virginia," he repeated. "A beautiful state."

"Yes, it is," Mama said.

"Are you in Key West on business or pleasure?" Tony Curtis asked.

"Oh, it's just a vacation," Mama said.

"Actually, my parents are trying to patch up their marriage," I blurted out. All of a sudden I was determined to spill the beans, to tell Tony Curtis the *whole thing*. He had such a good marriage himself that maybe he could fix up Mama and Daddy's, give them some good Hollywood advice—a hot tip from the stars.

"Jenny, don't you dare!" Mama shrieked.

Tony Curtis looked very surprised. "Well," he said, inching back, "I was going to say, if you've got the time, and if you're interested, we'll be shooting crowd scenes for the next two days, and we need extras. Your daughter"—he rolled those big blue eyes at *me*—"might get a kick out of being in the movie."

I threw my book on the floor and started jumping up and down. "In the movie? I'd *love* to be in the movie!"

Behind the desk, Hal started laughing.

"It's a deal, then," Tony Curtis said to Mama. "You and your husband can be in it, too, ma'am, if you want to see what it's all about. Just show up at the Navy dock tomorrow morning at nine. We need a big civilian crowd to wave hello at the submarine when it comes into the port."

"All right," Mama said. You could barely hear her.

Tony Curtis left for good then, waving to me from the door before he spun militarily on his heel and vanished into the shrubbery. I gathered up his cigarette butts from the ashtray, for my collection.

"Maybe you'll be discovered." Hal winked at me.

"Oh, don't be silly," Mama said. "Don't give her any ideas."

But I already had ideas. Why not? Jean Seberg, the daughter of an Iowa druggist, had been picked from eighteen thousand hopefuls to be Joan of Arc.

"Anyway, who knows?" Mama flung back over her shoulder to Hal. "Maybe *I'll* be discovered!"

RAN ALL THE way to our rooms, Mama following. Daddy sat in one of the wicker armchairs, reading in a yellow pool of light from the Chinese lamp with the tassels. The rest of the room was dark. A drink sat sweating on the glass table beside him. Overhead, in the darkness, the fan went around and around, making a whispery noise like wind in the fields at home.

"Daddy, Daddy, Daddy! Guess what? You'll never believe it! We get to be in the movie!" I stood panting just inside the door.

Daddy looked up at me very slowly then, as if he were coming back from somewhere far away, as if I were speaking a foreign language. In the light from the Chinese lamp, his face looked haunted, lined, and old; his eyes were bleak and dark in their deep sockets. My heart went down to my feet. I had caught Daddy out, surprised him. This was the way he *really* felt, and all the fishing trips and good deeds in the world could never change it.

"What is it, Jenny?" he said.

I had to say it, to blunder on. "All of us—you and Mama

and me—get to be in the movie tomorrow if we go down to the docks. They need extras. Tony Curtis said."

Daddy looked at me. I realized that the last thing in the world he'd ever want to do was be in a movie. He put a piece of paper in the book to mark his place, and put the book on the table.

"Come on, Daddy, *please* can we do it?"

A gray smile came and went at the sides of his mouth. "Well, honey, *of course* you and your mother can go down there—"

In the middle of that sentence, I felt his attention shift away from me, and I realized he was speaking now to Mama, who must have come in behind me as he spoke. "—but I believe I'll pass on it."

"John—" Mama was still breathless from her climb up the stairs. "John, come on, this is the chance of a lifetime."

"Mr. Kinney has sent me some figures I have to look over in the morning." Daddy's face was gray, his long cheeks shadowy and hollow.

Of course. How *could* he do it? I thought. How could he? A man who voted for Adlai Stevenson and loved Carroll Byrd? A man whose own father had killed himself? Of course he couldn't do it.

Behind me, Mama started to cry. I heard her ragged breathing and those snuffly sounds she always made. *Get a grip!* I wanted to scream at her. Didn't she understand him at all? Didn't she understand *anything*?

Daddy did not get up from the chair. "Jenny, go on to bed,"

he told me. "It's late. Go on, so you can be in the movie in the morning."

I spun around, pushing Mama aside. "I hate you!" I screamed from the balcony. "I hate you both!" I tore off into the dark and ran all the way to the cemetery, where I threw myself down on somebody's grave, and cried and cried and cried. The concrete was still warm from the sun; I could feel its heat down the length of my body. It felt strange, good. Finally I rolled over on my back and looked at the starry bowl of the sky. I took a deep breath. There was a full moon coming up, so I could see the white graves in their orderly rows, the palms, the urns, and all the angels. I would never be an angel. I knew that now. Mama was an angel, and Rayette was an angel, but I would never be one, not in a million years, no matter how many good deeds I did. I was suddenly *sick* of good deeds, and vowed never to do another one. They hadn't worked, anyway. Nothing had worked, and nothing was ever going to work. Mama and Daddy would never patch up their marriage. They would never get back together.

I would be an orphan, like Jane Eyre. I would wander alone in the world, doing bad deeds. I would become a stripper. A prostitute. A love slave. Who cared? Not Jesus, obviously, who hadn't done a damn thing for me in spite of all my efforts. I probably didn't even believe in Him, as a matter of fact. He was too damn picky. Too hard to please.

I lay on my back on top of a dead person, thinking this stuff.

Bats swooped around overhead. A cat stole up to rub against

my drooping arm, and I petted it till it purred. The longer I stayed there, the brighter the moonlight grew, and the more I could see. I could see everything.

It was after midnight when I got back to the Blue Marlin, where I found Mama and Daddy and Mr. Rudy and a young Cuban policeman all sitting around in room 209 waiting for me. They jumped up when I came in.

"Oh, thank goodness! Oh, thank God!" Mama rushed over to smother me in tears and Chanel No. 5.

Daddy said, "I guess we won't be needing your services after all," and shook hands with the young Cuban policeman, who left looking disgusted. Mr. Rudy clicked his tongue disapprovingly at me before he slipped out the door, too.

"I'm sorry," I started, though I wasn't, but Daddy put his finger to my lips. "Hush, Jenny. It's all right. Just go to bed now, okay? It's late. We'll talk about this in the morning."

B
UT IN THE morning there was no time to talk. Mama woke me by shaking my shoulders and saying, "Jenny! Jenny! Come on, get up! We're going to be in the movie! Wake up, honey, you'll want to wash your hair—" I opened my eyes to find her sitting on the edge of my bed looking as beautiful as any movie star, hair fixed just so, fire-engine-red lips smiling. She wore a fresh dose of perfume and a full skirted red-flowered dress.

"You look beautiful, Mama," I said.

"Come on, Jenny, hurry." Daddy stood behind her. He was dressed for the movie, too, in a clean white shirt and khaki pants. I didn't ask any questions. I jumped up and took a shower and put on my middy-blouse outfit and some of Mama's dusting powder. I parted my hair and combed it carefully, and made spit curls over my ears. Then I put on a whole lot of Mama's makeup, turning the corners of my eyes into silver points like shark fins, like angel wings. Mama and Daddy looked at each other but did not say a thing about my makeup.

They grabbed my hands and we set off down the street along with the crowd. People poured out of motels and shops and restaurants—tourists, tramps, artists, merchants and shop-girls, and women wiping their hands on their aprons. Even the iguana man fell in, with his big lizard circling his shoulders. It was a holiday. "*Buenos días*, Jenny," called Luisa, mincing along in yellow short shorts and high heels. Sleepy-eyed Rosa waved. Mama's eyebrows made little arches of surprise. She jerked my hand. "Jenny, who *are* those girls?" But I didn't have to answer, because somebody started singing: "You had a wife and forty-nine kids, but you *left*, you *left*, you *left*, right, *left*," and everybody took it up. We became a parade.

We trooped to the Navy yard and onto the docks, burst-ing into a spontaneous cheer at the sight of the pink subma-rine that steamed back and forth in the harbor, decks covered with actors. I had never seen it under way before. Against that bright blue water, the pink submarine was miraculous. Mama squeezed my hand. Pelicans and gulls wheeled overhead. Camera crews were everywhere: on a launch in the water, on an official-looking truck at the dock, on top of a warehouse. A man with a beard and a bullhorn was lifted high above us on a crane.

"Okay!" His amplified voice rang out. "Ladies and gentle-men! Boys and girls! We appreciate your participation here today! Now, all you have to do is cheer—" At this point, we drowned him out. He had to wave his arms back and forth to restore order. "Good! Very good! All you have to do is cheer—just like that—when the sub comes up to the dock. That's it! Got it?"

We cheered again. My throat was getting sore already, and it didn't even *count* yet.

"Okay! Now save it. Don't do it until I give you the sign. Then you start, and be sure to wave hello. These guys have been out in the Philippines winning a war for you, so you're glad to see them, right? Okay?"

I strained to see Tony Curtis on the deck of the submarine, but it was still too far away. The actors looked like ants. The director held his bullhorn up against the sky, then brought it down. Great puffs of white smoke shot out of the smokestacks as the pink sub headed toward shore, toward us, toward home. I started crying and couldn't stop. The crowd went wild. I could hear Mama's high voice, Daddy's piercing whistle. My makeup was running but I didn't care. I wiped silvery tears off my chin and kept on crying. It was the happiest moment of my life. We waved and cheered until the pink submarine was at the dock, and Tony Curtis looked straight at me, I swear he did, and winked.

So I DID it. I pulled it off. We stayed in Key West for an- other week, and every day Daddy softened up a bit more, relaxing into his old self again. I could see it happening. My parents paid more and more attention to each other, less to me. When the maid came to their room in the mornings, she had only one bed to make up. I was free to roam all over town by myself, free to get my ears pierced by the oldest of the Cu- ban children who lived over the grocery—an act which served to unite Mama and Daddy even more, *against* me: "Honestly, Jenny, nice girls in Virginia don't have pierced ears! Only *maids* have pierced ears, don't you know *anything*?" Mama wailed, clutching Daddy's hand for support. They would be together for twenty more years.

Though this ought to be the end of the story, it's not. One more thing happened. One more thing is *always* happening, isn't it? This is the reason I have found life to be harder than fiction, where you can make it all work out to suit you and put The End wherever you please. But back to the story.

A few days before we left for home, Caroline and Tom flew down to Key West for a weekend visit, bringing their brand-new baby (Thomas Kraft Burlington, Jr.—then called Tom-Tom) with them. I couldn't wait to see Tom Burlington again, especially now that I had gotten such a nice tan and a new haircut and had my ears pierced and did not have to be good anymore. I had *grown up,* I felt. I had been tongue-kissed, and lived among stars.

I was ready for him.

But when they arrived, Tom wouldn't pay a bit of attention to me, no more than Mason ever had. All he would do was wait on Caroline hand and foot, and make goo-goo eyes at his stupid little pointy-headed baby. It made me sick! Tom-Tom had colic, and spit up his milk, and cried all the time. I was dying to show Tom around Key West (I had not specifically invited Caroline), which I couldn't do until Tom-Tom fell asleep, which took forever. But finally he lay curled on his stomach in a little red ball, oohed and aahed over by Mama, and Tom stood up.

"Come on, honey," he said to Caroline. "Let's let Jenny give us this grand tour we've been hearing so much about."

I held my breath, but Caroline shook her head. "No, honey, you go on. I'll just catch a few winks myself, I think. I'm really tired."

Tom looked doubtful, but she squeezed his hand. "Go *on,* silly," she said, and he did.

I showed him the cemetery first, but he seemed preoccupied, and didn't even laugh at the funny tombstone that read

"I Told You I Was Sick." Instead he looked sweaty and pale, worried. "I ought to go back," he said.

"No, don't!" I was howling. "Come on. You've got to come down to the docks for the sunset. I want to show you the sharks and the iguana man."

Tom looked uncomfortable now. "Maybe tomorrow," he said, "when Caroline can come, too."

We stood there awkwardly among the tombs and angels, which I loved, while—for the second time in Tom's presence—I started crying uncontrollably. I don't know what I had thought—that he would say a poem to me in the graveyard, perhaps, something about love and death, or undying love . . . about his undying love for me. Now I knew I was a fool—an idiot.

I turned and took off running through the cemetery without another word.

"Hey!" Tom yelled behind me. "Jenny! Stop!"

But I wouldn't have stopped for anything. I ran like the wind, straight through the cemetery and out the gate and into the carnival bustle of late afternoon, all the way down Duval Street to the Havana Madrid, where I nearly crashed into Luisa's billboard. Here I stopped short, panting hard. The door to the bar stood wide open, dark and inviting.

I walked in.

It took a while for my eyes to adjust, but then I could see fine. It was plenty light where the sailors sat with their beers, looking up at a girl who walked the long shiny bar wearing nothing but pasties and a G-string, stopping from time to time to dangle her breasts in their faces. She was a big-legged Cuban girl, nobody I had ever seen before. While I watched, she reached out and grabbed a sailor's hat and rubbed it between her legs while he turned bright red and started grabbing for it. "Gimme that!" he said. "Give it back!" No older-looking than Harlan Boyd, he was mortified. Everybody was laughing at him when the girl smacked the hat back on his head and swayed off down the long bar and exited. I peered at the girls and men sitting at the tables all around the sawdust floor, looking for Rosa and Luisa, but I didn't see them. The unimaginable corners of the cavernous room were dark and vast.

"Are you lost, Miss?" a tall black man at my elbow asked.

"I just came in for a drink," I said, and went over to the bar and climbed up on a wooden stool before he could stop me. Two men sitting to my left elbowed each other, grinning at me. They were old and fat. I grinned back. "Well, hello there, honey," one of them said. A skinny redhead sashayed down the bar in a top-hat-and-tails outfit, then came back without the tails.

I knew exactly what Jesus would think of this place, but since he didn't exist anyway, I ordered a coke from the flat-chested blonde bartender, who was wearing a sort of corset.

"Make that a rum and Coke for the little lady," the man said, and the bartender raised an eyebrow at him but brought it. I took a big drink. The man scooted his stool closer to mine. He touched my knee lightly, with one finger.

"Thank you, this is a delicious cocktail," I said.

"It is, huh!" And suddenly Red is there, too, the other bartender, hands on substantial hips, fiery Medusa hair standing out all around her head, bosom heaving furiously. "Jenny, you get your ass out of here *right now*!" she yells, and I run out the door, straight into Tom Burlington. He grabs my shoulders and shakes me until my teeth rattle, then hugs me, then shakes me again.

"You little bitch!" he says.

What a relief! I have been recognized at last. I *am* a little bitch, and I will never be an angel, and it's okay. I start laughing, and Tom starts laughing, too.

This is the moment when the street photographer snapped our picture, and Tom paid him for it, and gave it to me, and I have it still. I blew it up. I tend to move around a lot, but I always take this picture with me, and keep it right here on my desk.

In the picture, Tom Burlington and I cling together in the jostling crowd, our arms wound tightly around each other. We look like lovers, which we never were. Behind us is the Havana Madrid sign with the winking lady's face on it. There is something she knows that I don't know yet. But I will learn. And I will get my period, and some breasts. I will also *do it* plenty, thereby falling into numerous messy situations too awful to mention here. I will never be really good again. I am not good. I am as ornery and difficult and inconsolable as Carroll Byrd.

I don't know whatever happened to her, or to Tom Burlington, who left my sister for another woman, an English teacher at his school, when Tom-Tom was still small. Caroline is happily remarried now, to a lawyer in Charleston, South Carolina, where she has raised four children and is the head of the Historical Society. Our lives are very different, Caroline's and mine, and I regret that I don't see much of her now, except for her children's graduations and weddings. My oldest sister Beth is still married and still living out west; I don't see much of her, either. Tony Curtis and Janet Leigh are long divorced. He's an artist now. Cary Grant is dead. Grandmother and Aunt Chloë and Aunt Judy are dead. Mama is dead, too, of ovarian cancer in 1979. After she died, Daddy turned the mill into a co-op and gave it to his employees; Mr. Kinney's son is running it today. Then Daddy surprised everybody by moving to Boca Raton, Florida, where he "up and married" (as Mama would have said) the real estate woman who sold him his condo. This woman has a black spiky hairdo, and everybody calls her "The Shark." Daddy takes Elderhostel courses and seems very happy; his current personality bears no relation, that I can see, to his former self, to the person who is in this story. Cousin Glenda ran a rest home for many years after Raymond's death; now she is *in* the rest home, and Rayette and her husband are running it. Rayette sends me a long chatty Christmas letter every year, even though I never did get a grip. I don't know what happened to Harlan Boyd. Jinx is still my friend, and we keep in touch by phone, and meet at a spa in Sedona once a year.

For some reason, I can't quit writing this story, or looking at this picture, in which the sun is so bright, and Tom Burlington and I are smiling like crazy. I guess it reminds me of Mama and Daddy in love, of the day when Mama and Daddy and I walked down to the docks to be in the movie, and cheered when the pink submarine came in, and waved hello.

─────The Geographical Cure─────

I T MAKES ME so happy to hold this little book in my hands—
for of all the stories I've ever written, this one is dearest to
me, capturing the essence of my own childhood—the kind
of unruly, spoiled only child I was; the sweetness of my troubled parents; and the magical essence of Key West, one of
my favorite places in the world ever since January 1959, when
these events actually occurred.

Or did they? Well, not *all* of them, because this is autobio-
graphical *fiction*, actually, with the emphasis on fiction.

So what's the difference? Let me explain. During a lifetime
of writing, I have always felt that I can tell the truth better
in fiction than nonfiction. Real life is often chaotic, mysterious, unfathomable. But in fiction, you can change the order of
events, emphasize or alter certain aspects of the characters—
you can even create new people or take real people away in an
instant. That means you can instill some sort of order to create
meaning, so that the story will make sense—where real life so
often does not. Fiction is also a heightened reality—you "up
the ante" in order to grab the reader's attention and hold it,
increasing or emphasizing the conflict, adjusting the pace of

the story accordingly, often making it conform to the old tried and truly satisfying plot sequence of beginning, middle, end.

So this story is fiction, okay?

My own father, Ernest Smith of Grundy, Virginia, did *not* have an affair with Carroll Byrd or anybody else that I know of. Carroll Byrd, the "other woman" in this story, is pure fiction, just a type I admired and wanted to be as a girl and was not: artistic, unconventional. My sweet daddy, a workaholic storekeeper, was "kindly nervous," as he put it, his own euphemistic term for bipolar illness, or "manic depression" as it was then called. But the manic phase was no fun for him—no elation, no wild sprees—instead he just worked harder than ever at his dimestore until these weeks of intense activity led inevitably to a downward spiral. He'd talk less and less, stay in bed more and more, finally "going off" someplace to get treatment—such as Highland Hospital in Asheville, N.C., or Silver Hill in New Canaan, Ct., where he had been hospitalized for about six months in 1958 when this story begins.

My beautiful mother, Virginia Marshall Smith, "kindly nervous" herself, was simultaneously being treated for anxiety and depression at the University of Virginia hospital in Charlottesville. So I was sent to stay with my Aunt Millie and Uncle Bob in Maryland—but let me assure you that my sophisticated Aunt Millie (Martinis! League of Women Voters!) was *not* Cousin Glenda in this story; in fact she was the polar opposite of Cousin Glenda. I just made Glenda up, feeling that I needed some humor at this point and using some of the tropes of the time such as car coats, bomb shelters, "What would Jesus think?" and "Get a grip!"

But it is true that our own nervous little nuclear family was indeed separated for many months during 1958; and it is also true that upon discharge my father's physician at Silver Hill Hospital prescribed not only lithium for him but also a Geographical Cure for their Marriage, now apparently "troubled" in some way that nobody would explain to me, though I would participate in this Geographical Cure—a big long trip! Daddy chose Key West, Florida, for the Geographical Cure because he had been stationed there in the Navy and loved it. He and Mama had apparently been back to Key West once before (before I was born! I couldn't even imagine this—life without me! It gave me a sick headache; I had to take a Goody Powder and go right to bed).

But the Geographical Cure did not seem to be working as my father drove our big white fishtail Buick endlessly down the eastern seaboard that January of 1959, seldom speaking except for things like Mama saying, "Lee, will you please tell your daddy to stop for more cigarettes?" which I would dutifully repeat even though he was sitting right there, or me screaming "Can't we go to Weeki Wachee Springs? Please please please!" as the billboard flashed past, for I planned to be a professional mermaid when I grew up. Nothing doing. We pressed on in the smoke-filled car. I felt like the Marriage was a fourth passenger, sitting glumly next to me in the back seat.

Each night in the series of little tourist cottages was grim, with Mama and me in one bed and Daddy in the other, and several times I awakened to see his bent shadow outside the window, pacing back and forth. What if he had another breakdown? What if the marriage couldn't be cured?

But I loved that final part of the drive, with the luminous sea and sky surrounding us and the Keys with their wonderful names: Key Largo, Cudjoe, Sugarleaf, Saddlebunch, Raccoon.

"We're almost there," Daddy said.

Mama reapplied her lipstick, Revlon Fire and Ice.

And finally we were in Key West—the scruffiest, wildest place I had ever seen, a bright buzz of noise and color. We turned left off Truman Avenue onto Duval Street, and now I could glimpse a shining patch of ocean. Daddy pulled into a motel named the Blue Marlin with a huge fish on its sign. Mama and I waited in the car while he headed for the office. The motel was made of blue concrete, two stories in a U-shape around a good-size pool with a diving board and a slide. Perfect for a mermaid.

Finally Daddy got back in the car with a funny look on his face. "Girls, you're not going to believe this," he said slowly.

"What? What is it? Is it bad news from home?" Mama's pretty face was an instant mask of alarm.

"Oh no, nothing like that." Daddy really smiled for the first time on the trip. "It appears that this entire motel has been taken over by the cast and crew of a movie that they are shooting on location right now in Key West, over at the Navy Yard. There are only four rooms that they're not occupying, and now we've got two of them. They asked me a lot of questions. I had to swear that we weren't journalists or photographers in order to stay here. And Lee," he added in a no-nonsense voice, "I promised that you would not bother the stars. Do you hear me? Or the crew, or anybody else."

"Which stars?" Mama hardly breathed. She was already in heaven.

"Well, there's Dina Merrill," Daddy said, "and Tony Curtis."

"Tony Curtis!" Mama and I squealed together. We pored over the *National Enquirer*, the *Midnight Star*, and countless other movie magazines that we read cover to cover. Every week when the movie changed at the Lynwood Theater downtown, we were right there in our favorite seats, tenth-row aisle, clutching our Baby Ruths.

"And that's not all," Daddy said.

"Who?" we shrieked.

"Cary Grant."

"Cary Grant!" We couldn't believe it. The most gorgeous, the most elegant, the biggest star in Hollywood. "The man at the desk says he's a real gentleman," Daddy said. I was not so sure of that, thinking of his recent love affair with Sophia Loren. Mama and I knew everything.

Thus it began, though most of this book is my own creation.

As for the movie itself, *Operation Petticoat* featured a real pink submarine, anchored out in the ocean off Key West. Its flimsy plot involves a navy lieutenant commander (Cary Grant) and his con man executive officer (Tony Curtis) who must take the fictional damaged sub USS *Sea Tiger* into a seedy dockyard for repair during World War II, rescuing a crew of stranded army nurses on the way. The only available paint for repair is red and white (hence the sub's pink color), and the only available bunks for the nurses are down in the submarine's tight quarters (wink, wink). The film takes place during the Battle of the Philippines in the opening days of the United States involvement in World War II. Some elements of the screenplay were taken from actual incidents that happened with some of the Pacific Fleet's submarines during the war, though points of historical accuracy are few. Most filming was done in and around Naval Station Key West, now known as the Truman Annex of Naval Air Station Key West.

Operation Petticoat was a huge box-office hit, the #3 moneymaker of 1960, earning $6,800,000—just behind #1 *Psycho* and #2 *Ben-Hur*. The review in *Variety* was typical: "*Operation Petticoat* has no more weight than a sackful of feathers, but it has a lot of laughs. Cary Grant and Tony Curtis are excellent, and the film is directed by Blake Edwards with a slam-bang pace." Cary Grant's residuals topped $3 million, making it his most profitable film to date. The film was the basis for a TV series in 1977.

The Geographical Cure worked. Mama and Daddy would go home refreshed, and stay married for the rest of their lives. He would run his dimestore for thirty-three more years. Surrounded by the stars in Key West, Mama pepped right up and was soon wearing high-heel sandals and a pink hibiscus in her hair. Daddy went deep-sea fishing with a guy named Captain Tony and played poker with the film crew. Every night at 7:00 p.m., Mama and I seated ourselves on a rattan love seat in the lobby of the Blue Marlin pretending to read newspapers while we eavesdropped on Tony Curtis's daily call from the public telephone to Janet Leigh back in Hollywood, which always ended with Tony's words, "God bless you, my darling!" We rattled our newspapers emotionally. One day at the pool, Tony Curtis offered me a package of cheese nabs; I would save it for decades. Near the end of the second week, one of the directors asked our family if we would like to be in the movie. "You bet!" I cried out. "Oh, brother," Daddy said. But there we were, and there we still are to this day in the giant crowd on the Key West dock when the pink submarine comes into port at the end of the movie, cheering and waving hello.

Lee Smith
January 10, 2020